# Who's Toni Rice?

---

By

Lisa A. Forrest

*To the understanding that*

*there is always light after the darkness…*

*Especially when*

*you learn to utilize those dark experiences*

*to help others.*

*~L.A.F.~*

## Acknowledgement

I would like to take this moment to acknowledge my inspiration for this book. **Mr. Steve Merricks**... I Thank You for your wonderful imagination, and your endless humor. I'm sure that you remember the day that you came up with the idea and insinuation of **Agent-62**. It was a wonderful, creative and exciting accusation that fueled my imagination and the main characters for "Who's Toni Rice?"

Steve and I grew up in the same neighborhood of Frankford, in Philly. We went to the same elementary school, A.M. Stearne, and were in the same grade. I was a shy, quiet girl who was about my schoolwork and I remember him as one of the cute, nice kids. We reconnected on Facebook a few months back and did some catching up, along with a few other fun activities. *Wink wink* Those few weeks left me a lifetime of memories, including the inspiration for this novel. I would like to say,

'Thank you, Mr. Merricks, for your lively imagination and beautiful spirit! Our time together has fueled a life-long friendship, and definitely memories that will last for the rest of my life. Thanks again dear friend.'

--Agent-62

# Preface

We all have heard the saying that we are the product of our environment. We are also the product of our experiences, especially our childhood experiences. As we grow and mature, we can let our negative experiences mold our lives towards negativity or choose to use those experiences for positivity. We can allow them to thrust us into a negative world of drama and danger, or we can choose to let them guide us and allow them to inspire our drives to success.

We live in a complicated world. We have to choose which part we play in the evolution of our time here. Positive change, many times, requires dark choices. Not all people are built to choose the darkness to get to the light. Some people have been protected and exposed to mostly the best of what life offers. This allows for a mostly positive outlook on life and many times a good life's experience.

Then there are those who experience a living hell. And in order for those people to see the good in the world, they need help to recognize the cause of their own darkness, in order to see the beauty of life's experiences. Overcoming the darkness is crucial to this growth. But the darkness of the past can also be the special part of you to help to conquer the darkness's in life for others, and sometimes even... The World —

#WhosToniRice

# Who's Toni Rice?

*The Range.*

A tall, physically fit, dark-skinned man with locs, enters the lobby of the gun range. He speaks to a couple of members who he's familiar with, then stops at the front desk to chit-chat with the receptionist about setting up a new schedule to bring some of his mentee's in for target practice. Once he's finished, he walks back to the shooting area to get his practice in.

As he goes back to get to an open firing lane, he walks past a young woman who he couldn't help but notice. She's holding her weapon impeccably and her stance is perfect. He stops to watch her as she shoots with a marksman's aim. He can hardly take his eyes off her but realizes that he may seem a bit creepy to her if he continued to stare and she caught him.

*She* is a tall, brown skinned, medium build woman with natural hair that has blondish brown definitions throughout her beautifully defined curl pattern; *He* loved natural hair on Black women.

As he resumes walking by, he thinks to himself how taken he is by her physique and style; he hasn't seen her face yet. Her well fitted jeans, along with her black leather boots and black tee shirt shows a subtle style that gave him the feeling that she liked to dress well. He wants to try to keep his eye on her, so that he can introduce himself before she leaves, but he becomes so immersed in his own target practice that he doesn't see her leave.

He is very disappointed as he ends his own practice and walks out of the shooting area, hoping to catch up with her before she leaves. He doesn't see her, so he begins to ask questions about her. He has been practicing at this range for years, so he has no problem with the people who work here giving him information. He is told that her name is Toni Rice and that she is a new instructor at the range. He asks a lot of questions that they can't answer.

As he is leaving, he happens to see Toni walk out of the building. She has been in a meeting with the range master about her schedule and her trainee's. He had only seen her from the back, so he recognized her clothes and her hair as she walked out. He couldn't wait to introduce himself, so he walked over to her.

"Hello there, young lady! I couldn't help but notice you in there. You're quite the marksman."

When Toni turned around, he was excited by her beauty. He was initially attracted to her skill, her physique, her style and her aura. Her facial beauty is an added surprise. He extended his hand,

"My name is Yusuf, and yours?"

Toni just looked at him and hesitated to answer the tall, fit, ebony man, with his flawless, well-groomed locs. He had average looks, but attractive just the same. She didn't feel anything threatening about him, so she extended her hand to shake his, with a strong, firm grip.

"I'm Toni."

"Well, good morning Ms. Toni! I'm pleased to meet you!"

"Good morning."

"So, how did you become such a sharpshooter, if you don't mind me asking?"

"Practice."

Yusuf laughed at the obviousness of her answer and got the feeling that she wanted no parts of him. He decided to end the conversation there and looked forward to running into her again with, hopefully, a bit more of a friendly interaction.

"Okay, well it was nice meeting you! And welcome to the range. I hope to see you here again. We need more of us as instructors and learning how to shoot and shoot well. Have a wonderful day, Toni!"

"You too."

Yusuf walked to his car feeling a bit disappointed that he didn't get the connection that he'd hoped for with such a fascinating woman. He rarely experienced the strong attraction that he had, to someone he didn't know, but there was something about her. He couldn't wait to run into her again, in order to break the ice with her.

About a week later, he came to the range again and saw her training a member. He just walked by her to get to his own practicing lane and felt a brief excitement as he walked past. And it didn't help that her perfume smelled wonderful. He wouldn't bother her while she was instructing, but he wanted to try to stay aware enough to know when she was finished with her trainee.

He got into his own practice, but every time he finished a firing round, he peaked to see if she was still there. After his fourth round of shooting, he looked over to where she was, and she was gone. He quickly left the shooting area to see if he could catch up to her.

He saw her in the lobby talking to another member of the range. He walked towards the counter and talked to the receptionist, waiting for the opportunity to speak to Toni and engage her in conversation. She finished up with the other member and Yusuf walked towards her to speak to her.

"Hello Toni! How are you today? It's nice to see you again!"

"Hello…" Toni hesitates because she forgot his name.

"Yusuf! My name is Yusuf."

"Oh yes, I'm sorry! Hello, Yusuf."

"How's it going as a new instructor?"

"It's awesome! I have some great students who learn pretty quickly."

"That's wonderful! Do you have more students today?"

"Yes, I do."

"Right away?"

"No, not for another hour."

That was the in that Yusuf needed.

"Cool! How about grabbing some coffee with me next door?"

"Um…" Toni thinks about it, then realizes that she could really use some coffee.

"Okay!" Says Toni.

She and Yusuf go next door to the coffee shop. It's not too crowded and didn't take long to get their coffee. They each grab their coffee, then sit down at a table.

"So, what made you want to be a shooting instructor?" Said Yusuf.

"I needed a job." Toni laughs at his question and her answer. Yusuf laughs too.

"Well, that's a good reason. What got you interested in shooting in the first place?"

"My parents were big on self-defense. They wanted to make sure that I could protect myself in any situation."

"Oh, really? What other types of self-defense are you trained in?"

"Many!" Toni didn't seem to want to fully answer the question. She wasn't sure of what his motives were and was naturally suspicious of people. She didn't want to give up too much information about herself. She decided to turn the tables.

"So, what is it that you do?"

"I'm sort of a community activist."

"Hmmm, so you practice shooting guns to prepare to shoot all the bad guys in your community?" Toni starts cracking up laughing. Yusuf doesn't find it funny.

"You're assuming that I live in a bad neighborhood. Don't you think that's a bit prejudiced? Where do you live?"

"None of your business and I was just being playful. How am I prejudiced if we're both African-American?"

"Oh, many of us are prejudiced against each other. Some of us who are better off and have never experienced living in the hood, have a lot of negative and stereotypical beliefs about the hood and people who live in the hood."

"Well, so you *do* live in the hood?"

"Yes, I do! And I will never leave. It's where I was born and raised. And it's where most of my family is. There's no shame for me to live in my hometown. I chose to stay and try to rebuild my community, instead of leaving to go live in the suburbs. As an activist, I have a lot of plans to educate the people in my community, about their rights and community economics. And to also rebuild the infrastructure."

"How noble of you!" Said Toni in an almost sarcastic response, but she caught herself.

"So, what made you want to become sort of a community activist; your words?"

Yusuf was getting the feeling that she was a bit snobbish, but he wanted to give her the benefit of the doubt, so he continued with his answer.

"Well, I left to go away to college and I actually lived in Compton after college with my then girlfriend. It didn't work out but living there is what gave me the idea to come back home and rebuild my own community. We were doing community work there and it was making a difference for some of those kids and the residents."

"Oh, cool!" Toni looks at the time on her cell phone.

"Well, it's time for me to get back to work. Maybe I'll see you next time." She smiled at Yusuf as she got up.

"Well, I was hoping that maybe we could go out some time." Yusuf got up too.

"Okay. I'll think about it. I'll let you know the next time that I see you." Toni starts walking away.

"Well, how about if I give you my number? You can just let me know in a text."

"I'm in a hurry right now, so maybe next time."

Yusuf didn't want to be too pushy, so he just left things there. He knew that he would see her again, soon.

***Charity and Cheesesteaks.***

After running into each other several times at the range, Toni eventually agreed to hang out with Yusuf. He decided to expose her to what he does, so he picked her up from the range and took her with him to a "Back to School" drive. They went to give out book bags and school supplies to the children in the neighborhood. Yusuf chose to do this for all the children in the neighborhood, not just the ones who were needy. He knew that children didn't understand those things, so he made it clear that *all* kids were invited.

Toni had never done any type of charity work. She had never been around people, who she was aware of, that couldn't buy school supplies for their children; this was a new experience for her. As she helped to give out the supplies to the children, she saw how excited each of them were to get *School Supplies*! She never really thought about it before, even though she would see charity events like this in the news sometimes. She had never been in need of anything growing up. But the rewarding feeling she received from the excitement and gratitude of the children felt great and was also surprising to her.

Once everything was over, Toni helped with the cleanup. Afterwards, Yusuf took her to a steak shop to get a cheesesteak. He claimed they were the best in the city.

"I don't know about all that! I may be from the burbs, but I've been in the city enough to know that Dalessandro's has the best cheesesteaks in the city."

"WHAT??? You *must* be crazy! Everybody knows that Max's has the best cheesesteaks in Philly!"

"Well, I don't know everybody, but everybody that I do know, knows that Dalessandro's is the best in the city. Hands down!"

"*Get* the hell outta hear! Have you ever even had a steak from here?"

"No! But I don't need to. I've had the best cheesesteaks in Philly. And you know the saying... 'Once you've had the best, aint no need for the rest!' or something like that."

Toni cracks up laughing, because she knew her quote was a bit off, but she also knew that she has eaten from the best cheesesteak joint in Philly.

Toni and Yusuf are in line debating over who has the best cheesesteaks, when Yusuf orders his...

"Cheesesteak, fried onions, mustard and ketchup."

Then Toni orders hers...

"Cheesesteak, fried onions, mustard, ketchup and mayo."

"Mayo?" Yusuf is insulted. "Who the hell puts mayo on a cheesesteak?"

"I do! And I know other people who do!"

"What the fuck? You and your friends know how to fuck up a real cheesesteak!"

Yusuf shakes his head.

"Mannn, you should be able to put whatever you want on a cheesesteak. Everybody has their own different tastes for things."

"Nah, that's because you and your friends get cheesesteaks from the wrong place, otherwise you wouldn't need no nasty ass mayo on it."

"Well, you're calling it nasty, so that's why you're so against it. You're prejudiced against mayo."

"On my cheesesteak, yeah! I use it on other foods, but not no cheesesteak."

Toni puts her hand out towards Yusuf's face.

"WHATEVER MAN!"

"You corny!" Says Yusuf.

"No, you're corny!"

They continue their debate to the table as they wait for their steaks. Once their order is up, Yusuf goes up to get their cheesesteaks. He hands Toni hers along with a lot of napkins.

"Here! I know that you're going to make a mess." Yusuf laughs.

"As a matter of fact, you're probably right. I'm not trying to be cute eating a cheesesteak. I love food, so my goal is to enjoy it. Not to worry about the mess that I might make. How about that?" Toni snatches the napkins, with her pretense of being offended.

Yusuf isn't sure if he offended her or not, then Toni begins laughing. Yusuf is relieved and sits down to dig into his steak sandwich. Toni has already taken a bite of hers. They both are quiet as they enjoy each delectable bite.

"So, would you agree with me now?" Says Yusuf.

"Well, it is really good, but I still prefer Dalessandro's cheesesteaks."

"Like I said, you corny!" They both laugh.

Once they finish eating, Yusuf asks Toni if she minds if he stops by his place, before he takes her back to her car. She says she doesn't. Once they get there, Toni is impressed by how well kept the outside of his home is, including his front lawn. Once inside, she's even more amazed with his immaculate home. It didn't look like a bachelor's home.

"Nice place!" Says Toni.

"Thank you! Have a seat. I have to run upstairs for a few."

As Toni sat down and saw the magazines on his coffee table, she was fascinated by his choices. Psychology Today, Black Enterprise, Money, Forbes, American Legacy and Architectural Digest. She wasn't familiar with American Legacy, so she picked it up to see what it was about. She read that it was a magazine about African American history and culture. She became immersed in the content. Almost everything that she read, she was unfamiliar with.

She realized that her education on African American culture was very limited. Yusuf came back downstairs.

"What are you reading?"

"Oh! I picked up your American Legacy magazine. I have never heard of it."

"You can take it if you want. I've already read it."

"No, but maybe I'll pick one up later."

"Well, it's quarterly and the new one will be out soon."

"Maybe later."

"Okay, let me check on my rotty, real quick, and then we can go."

"You have a rotty? Let me meet him!"

"You like dogs, nice."

"I've been around dogs all my life growing up and rotty's are awesome family dogs."

Yusuf went back to get his dog from the back porch. Dagan was happy to see him. Yusuf grabbed him by his collar and walked him out to meet Toni.

"WOW! He's huge! And beautiful!" Toni slowly reaches her hand out for Dagan to smell her. She is aware that dogs sense fear, so she makes sure she doesn't exude any. Dagan sniffs her hand, then moves closer to sniff her.

"Yeah, I made sure that I got a full bred rottweiler. They messed the breed up in this country. I bought him as a puppy and his mother was a champion. He's AKC certified."

"He doesn't bark much, does he? I do remember that about rotty's, but when they do bark it can be scary." Toni laughs.

"Yeah, he has a deep, frightening bark for sure." Yusuf takes Dagan back to the back porch so that he and Toni can leave.

"Alright then. Let's go!"

Toni got up to leave with Yusuf, to take her to her car. Once they got back to the gun range parking lot, he opened the car door for Toni then gave her a hug before she got into her car.

"I enjoyed you today." Said Yusuf.

"You know what? I really enjoyed spending time with you too." Toni smiled up at Yusuf from her driver seat.

"Well, we'll have to do this again. Soon!"

"I agree!" Said Toni. "I'll see you soon." Yusuf watched as she drove off, then jumped into his car and took off.


*Black History.*

Yusuf invited Toni to a Black History contest and event. He worked with several children's programs in the neighborhood to have them write essays on someone who was prominent in Black History. About forty kids entered the contest and today was for the 5 finalists.

Toni decided to go because she had so much fun with Yusuf the last time. It was held at the Boys and Girls Club. Yusuf gave a speech about the importance of Black children knowing their history. The first child read an essay on Malcolm X. The second on W.E.B. Du Bois; the third, Frederick Douglas; the fourth, Dr. Martin Luther King Jr. and the fifth on Harriet Tubman. The essay on Malcolm X won.

Toni learned so much from the children's essays that she never knew. This became a conversation for her and Yusuf after the event. Yusuf had prepared dinner for them earlier in the day. He just needed to add the finishing touches. He wanted Toni in the kitchen with him while he finished up. She sat at the breakfast bar, out of his way.

"I always thought that Malcolm X was bad person. I never liked him based on what I knew growing up." Said Toni.

"What? What the hell did you learn about him growing up? And from who?"

"I don't know. I didn't learn about him in school. I guess other people, maybe my parents, articles I read; I don't know. I just remember thinking of him as a bad guy. I guess it had to do with his involvement with the NOI too."

"OH! So, you know about the NOI?" Yusuf looked at Toni, surprised that she knew about the Nation of Islam.

"Yes, as a Black Nationalist organization."

"Oh, REALLY?"

"Yes! Everything that I knew about them was negative."

Yusuf laughed. "So, what did you think about the essay that the young man wrote? Do you feel the same about Malcolm?"

"Well, it said a lot of positive things about him, but we both know that there were many negative things about him."

"Oh, really!"

Yusuf explained to Toni many things about Malcolm's life that she was unaware of. He then suggested that she read "The Autobiography of Malcolm X" by Alex Haley. He knew that she would get a much greater understanding of his life from that book. She said that she'd pick it up but didn't know when she would have the time to read it.

Yusuf was almost in disbelief at Toni's ignorance of Malcolm X, but he realized that she was raised in the suburbs by a White father and Black mother. He kind of deduced that her mother must not have been very culturally aware. He was a teacher of his culture, so she became an accidental student. He would try to catch himself so that he wouldn't make her feel silly for not knowing more about her own culture. He was determined to educate her on the truth about Black culture, especially American Black culture.

Over the next few months, Yusuf would suggest many different books to Toni to help her to understand Black cultural history. He suggested "Before the Mayflower," "From Superman to

Man," "The Destruction of Black Civilization," "The Miseducation of the Negro," and "The Ethics of Identity." She devoured these books. She learned so much about being Black in America that she never really thought about. She had never experienced overt racism and never really related to other people's experience with it. She knew that it was real and that it happened, but she would sometimes think that many people pulled the race card way too much.

After reading all of the books that Yusuf suggested to her, she finally understood so much. Much of it enraged her as she realized all of the intentional programming and mistreatment. This gave her a fire to help Yusuf help the community. Most of their dates would start with a community event of some kind and Toni enjoyed every bit of it.

# I'm Digging You

*The Workout.*

Toni invited Yusuf to come workout with her at her gym. They did some basic workouts at first, then Toni got one of her self-defense partners to practice some kickboxing with her, but he wanted to practice some Krav Maga instead.

"Toni, let's practice Krav Maga, babe, it's been a while."

"Shhh… Not now, maybe later."

Toni looked over to see if Yusuf overheard her partner; he hadn't. He was talking to one of the boxers about his technique. So, she suggests to Yusuf to workout with the boxer while she and Jesse practices kickboxing.

"You kickbox? Let me see what you got?"

She laughs then says, "Maybe we can get it in after this warmup."

"Girl, be careful what you ask for."

Toni looks over her shoulder at Yusuf and winks. They both hooked up with their partners and practiced their kickboxing. Yusuf kept peaking over at Toni when he could. He was impressed. Then it was time for them to practice together. Yusuf was highly trained and didn't want to give Toni the full range of his skills. But he realized while practicing that she was really good. Once they finished practicing, he started being playfully suspicious.

"Are you sure the government didn't send you to spy on me? How rare is it that a female is this good at kickboxing? And why did you choose that particular gun range? And why are you my kind of fine and smart? Something aint right here."

At first Toni thinks that he's serious, but then he begins to laugh. She laughs with him.

"I'm really digging you! I have never met a woman like you before."

"Why thank you! That's a nice compliment. And for the record, I'm really digging you, too!"

Once they leave the gym, Toni wants to go home to shower; Yusuf followed. She only lives 15 minutes from her gym and has an apartment in the suburbs. Once they get there, Toni sets up one of her two bathrooms for Yusuf to take a shower. He goes back down to his car to get some fresh clothes. Toni waits until he gets comfortably in the shower before she jumps into the shower in her bedroom.

Yusuf finishes before her and hears her shower still running. Her bathroom door isn't fully closed, so he goes in, takes his towel off and puts it over the toilet seat. He then knocks on the shower door and opens it before Toni can respond. Toni doesn't say a word as he gets into the shower with her. They kiss intensely.

Yusuf grabs Toni's hand and leads her out of the shower. The water is still running. He sits on the towel covered toilet seat and guides Toni to his lap, facing him. He gently guides her to sit on him as he slides himself inside her, both still wet from the shower. Toni wraps her arms around his neck and begins to kiss him again. Yusuf wraps his arms around her waist as she slowly rocks back and forth on him.

The deeper they kiss, the faster she rocks back and forth until she can no longer maintain the kiss as she lets out her screams of pleasure. Yusuf lets out a few moans himself as he's enjoying her perfectly moist, warm wetness. It feels so good that he doesn't want it to end, so he changes his thoughts to maintain his erection without orgasming.

He wanted to make sure that Toni climaxed first; and she did. Once he felt her climax and let out her cry of satisfaction, he allowed himself to enjoy every bit of her wet warmth and the contraction of her orgasming vagina. His release was hard and soaking. They both embraced each other tightly as they enjoyed the moment of pleasure. They stayed in that position for a few minutes.

Toni pulled off of Yusuf and jumped back into the shower to finish up. Yusuf didn't think that it would be a good idea to jump back into Toni's shower, so he went into the other bathroom and showered himself again. He used another towel to dry himself off, then this time he got himself dressed. Toni did the same.

Once they finished up, they both jumped in their own cars and drove back to Yusuf's place. Toni parked her car on Yusuf's block.

She got into his car so that they could go to the supermarket together. He planned on cooking tonight.

**Not Today.**

Toni was waiting in the car for Yusuf. He had to run into the supermarket to pick up a few things, since he was fixing dinner tonight. She was sitting in the car listening to music with her eyes closed when she heard some kind of commotion going on. She looked in the rear-view mirror and it looked like some young females taunting an elderly lady.

Toni turned down the music in order to figure out what exactly was happening. She couldn't get a grasp on it, so she got out of the car.

"What's going on?" She said to the group of three females in about their early 20's and an elderly lady who looked to be about 75 years old.

"Mind your fuckin' business!" Shouted one of the young females.

"These stupid bitches think that because I'm old that I won't whip their asses! Come on, you fucking pieces of shit. I'll fuck you all up. COME ON!!!"

One of the girls tried to lunge at the old lady, but Toni intervened by stepping between them and putting her hand out to stop the girl.

"Not today, girlfriend!"

"I'm not your fucking girlfriend, now move the fuck outta my way, BITCH!"

Toni just stared at her with no intentions of moving. The elderly lady was in the back spewing all kinds of profanities at the females, to the point that Toni had to look back to see if she was really as old as she thought. She couldn't believe, what looked like, someone's grand or great grandmother would talk like that.

As Toni turned around to look at the old lady, the female who she stopped from charging the woman, walked back to the other two and convinced them to help her rush Toni, then the old lady. Toni was aware of their every step. So, when they tried to rush Toni, she put her hands out as she turned her head towards them, then pushed the first girl in the chest with all her body force. This pushed the other girls back too as they all fell to the ground. Toni then bent over and punched the first girl in the jaw three times in quick succession, and three times her head bounced on the ground. She then popped up to take care of the other two, but they began to yell that they were sorry, with one of the girls' hand extended trying to keep Toni away from them.

The elderly lady was still in the background cussing at them and laughing at the first girl who was still laying on the ground holding her broken jaw. Toni wasn't sure what her story was, but felt whatever it was, three young girls should never try to harm an elderly lady for any reason. She felt they should have walked away, even if she was in the wrong. Elderly people have earned their respect just by living to even become elderly. If she has mental issues, and Toni felt that she did based on her behavior, that would be all the more reason to walk away.

Toni backed up, away from the females. The one with the broken jaw was helped up by the other two and they all walked away. The old lady was still cussing and carrying on. Toni offered to take her home, but the old lady cussed her too. She was still cussing as she walked away, out of the parking lot, and up the street.

Yusuf was inside when he saw a group of people run to the window hollering "FIGHT!" He just shook his head and had no interest in watching it. He figured if it were still going on when he went out there, he would intervene. As he was getting wrung up, he heard a couple of people yelling "DAMN! She fucked her UP!" He then thought about Toni being out there, then moved a little faster to see what was going on. As he finished up in line, the people who were watching from the window were walking back into the supermarket.

As Yusuf walked out, he didn't see any signs of an altercation. Toni was back in the car with the music on, the three females were already out of sight, along with the elderly lady. Yusuf opened the car door.

"Did you see the fight?" Said Yusuf.

"What fight?" Said Toni.

"I don't know, but when I was in line, everybody was running to the window watching some fight that was going on." He looked at Toni. "You didn't see *anything*?"

"No, I was sitting here listening to music with my eyes closed."

"Woman, you better start paying better attention! Somebody could've been trying to car jack you or something, and you're busy listening to some damn music with your eyes closed. You're in the hood now, so you better act like it."

"Okay, baby! I'm sorry that I missed the fight. And next time I'll either turn off the music and pay attention or put up the windows and lock the doors."

"That sounds more like it, baby!" Said Yusuf as Toni leans over and pecks him on the lips. He smiles about being called baby by Toni and the peck on the lips, then starts the car and pulls off.

### Fried Chicken and Potato Salad.

Yusuf is in the kitchen cooking up a meal, while Toni is in the living room reading his American Legacy magazine. She always learns so much when she reads it. Yusuf banned her from the kitchen so that he could focus on dinner. He didn't need any sexy interruptions.

He was making fried chicken, potato salad, collard greens, candied sweet potatoes, macaroni and cheese, and cornbread. He wanted to make a culturally traditional meal for Toni to experience. He had already made the sweet potato pie that morning.

He set the dining room table up for them to eat. He called Toni in to join him.

"I made a traditional meal for us, since you've been so deprived of your culture. I hope that you enjoy it."

Toni laughed, then said, "It looks good, but I've had all this stuff before."

"Oh really? Who cooked it?"

"Stop acting like I'm so culturally unaware."

"It's not an act. You're not very culturally aware."

"WHATEVER!"

Yusuf just laughs at her self-denial. They begin to eat. Toni really enjoys his cooking.

"Oh, wow! This is really good, Yusuf! You're a great cook and you're right, I haven't tasted cooking like this before. It's delicious!"

"Thanks babe!"

Toni can't get enough. She eats so much that she's stuffed and can't eat a piece of his sweet potato pie, but Yusuf is sure to save her a few slices. After dinner, Toni helps Yusuf clean up and helped with the dishes. They would get into a conversation about Nat Turner that carried over to the living room when they were done cleaning up.

Toni couldn't understand how a man who killed women and children could be considered a hero. Yusuf explained the effects of the violence and oppression of slavery, and also the art of war. Nat Turners hand was forced based on the effects of slavery on him and the people around him. He did what he needed to do, even with the threat of knowing that death would probably be the result. Living as a slave was no longer his destiny. Toni kind of understood what he was saying.

Yusuf was enjoying Toni so much; he didn't want her to leave.

"I want you to stay over." Said Yusuf.

"I didn't bring a change of clothes, babe."

"Just leave a little early in the morning. I'd really like it if you stayed. I love your company. And I want a repeat of that feeling I got from you this afternoon." Yusuf winked at Toni, then she smiled back at Yusuf.

"Alright, babe. I'll stay."

Yusuf grabbed Toni and hugged her as he swayed back and forth. They sat on the couch for a couple more hours and continued to talk about Nat Turner, slavery, and the effects of slavery on modern times. They were both ready to wind down after their talk and went upstairs to shower and go to bed. With all the happenings of the day, they both realized they were too tired to do anything but sleep, so sleep they did.

The next morning, they were able to get a little sex session in before Toni had to leave. It was a nice way to start the day for them both. Toni left to go home and get dressed for the day. Yusuf had some community work to do early in the day.

*Meeting.*

Yusuf had a meeting with a few of the block captains and other community members, about a group of drug dealers who hung out on their blocks; they were from the same drug gang.

"Do any of you recognize any of these guys?" Asked Yusuf.

The block captains gave a collective "No."

No one recognized any of the dealers. Yusuf had moved the dealers who were from the neighborhood, out of the neighborhood with the help of family members of those dealers. This would be a harder task because these were unfamiliar faces and people. A few of them bought a house on one of the blocks together, so some of them lived there. The others were friends of theirs who came from other neighborhoods.

Yusuf developed a relationship with the dealers who moved out and whose families still lived in the neighborhood. He contacted a few of them to enlist their help to find out who these new dealers were and how dangerous they might be. So, a few of them drove through the hood with tinted windows to help identify the crew. They all recognized this group as rivals and really bad guys. They also offered to run them out, but Yusuf didn't want a turf war. He had to figure out another way.

He went to talk to the guy who was identified as the leader and one of the owners of the home. He left his car at the opposite end of the block so that they wouldn't get too antsy. Yusuf was also strapped with a couple of weapons. He approached the leader.

"What's up man! Can I talk to you for a minute?" Said Yusuf.

"Who the fuck are you?"

"That's that community guy who I was telling you about. The one who the neighbors were complaining to." Said one of the drug boys.

"What the fuck do you want, man?" Said the leader.

"I just want to talk to you for a minute."

"Go 'head! Start talking!"

"Can we talk to the side for a minute, bro?"

"FUCK no! We talk right here, or we aint talkin'!"

"Okay! Cool! I know who you are, and I know what you do..."

"And?"

"We work really hard to keep drugs off our streets. The last crew that was here just moved their shit somewhere else. I don't know where and I don't care where, just as long as it's not in my hood. I want to ask you to please do the same."

They all started laughing.

"You must be outta your fuckin' mind! You think I'm just gonna leave because you ask me too? Fuck outta here, PUSSY!"

Yusuf was prepared for such a response, so he had a back-up approach.

"Cool. So, here's the deal…"

"Deal? Nigga, if you don't get the fuck outta here with this bullshit… I'm gonna fuck you up!"

"If you don't leave the neighborhood on your own accord…"

One the drug boys walks up to Yusuf and swings at him. Yusuf ducks and uppercuts the guy and knocks him to the ground. A couple more guys try to rush him, but Yusuf is skilled in many martial arts and handles them all accordingly. The leader then pulls out his gun. Yusuf stands up with is hands up, paying attention to any moves to pull the trigger. The other guys back up.

"Get the fuck outta here, pussy! And don't come back here talkin' your dumb shit."

Yusuf doesn't say another word and backs up down the street, to his car. He then leaves, frustrated with the situation, but knowing that he now has to get the police involved. Something that he didn't want to do. He understood the system and was trying not to be the one to have young black men incarcerated. But he also had a program to help to intervene in that system. So, if any of the drug boys did get arrested, he had a program to try to help them turn their lives around. He just wasn't going to allow anyone to freely sell drugs in the neighborhood that he lived in, grew up in, protected and fought for.

He reluctantly got the police involved. They patrolled the streets where the house was, and they hung out there all day and night for a couple of weeks. This was a part of the program that Yusuf helped to develop and get funding for. The drug boys couldn't make their normal moves for those weeks, so they had to go elsewhere. They left the neighborhood after-all.

# Black Power

*Making Moves.*

Toni stopped by to see Yusuf, before going home from work; he was packing to go away. Toni was surprised that he didn't mention a thing to her.

"What's going on, babe? You going somewhere?"

"Yeah! I'm going out of town for a few days."

"Wow, you never mentioned anything to me. I could've gone with you."

"Nah, babe! I have to take care of some business."

"Well, where are you going?"

Yusuf laughed. "Why are you so nosey?"

"Nosey? I'm just asking where you're going. What's wrong with that?"

"Well, we're not there yet. We're still too new for me to tell you my every move, not that that would ever happen with anyone. There's a thing called trust that allows people in a relationship to give their partner a bit of freedom to do things without the need to question everything."

"But how do I ever get to a place of trust if you're being so secretive?"

"I don't know, but if it's something you can't handle, I understand. You'll have to weigh whether the relationship is worth it or not. And if I'm not, I get it. But for now, where I'm going and what I'm doing is my business. This isn't about another woman or anything like that. This is just some business that I need to take care of; that's it."

"Please don't insult me by treating me like a jealous girlfriend. That's not my concern, I promise you. But how do we get to a place of trusting each other if we're keeping secrets? You don't have to tell me your every more, or where you're going. But what's wrong with just letting me know that you were going out of town?"

"I just did!"

"Only because I walked in on you packing."

"Look! I was going to call you before I left. This was a last-minute thing. I got a call this morning, so there wasn't much time to inform you, okay? Now can I finish packing in peace?"

Toni just stared at him with a pissed look on her face. Yusuf looked back at her and laughed at her obvious disappointment. Toni just turned around to leave.

"Babe! Look! I'm sorry for the last-minute notice, but it's going to be like that sometimes."

Toni just left and slammed the door. Yusuf was tickled by her anger and was confident that she'd get over it.

-----

When Yusuf gets back a few days later, he gives Toni a call. She had been on his mind the entire trip.

"Hey babe, I'm back. I want to see you."

"I'm busy."

"Okay, well when can I see you?"

"I'm not sure. I'll call you."

"How are you? You were pretty mad at me the last time we saw each other."

"I'm over it."

"How are you?"

"I'm just fine."

Yusuf could tell that she is still pissed at him. Her conversation is cold and terse, but he would give her, her space.

"Okay, well hopefully we'll talk soon. Have a good day."

"You too."

The conversation ended there, and Toni and Yusuf wouldn't contact each other for a few days. Yusuf felt that it was getting silly, so he went to the gun range to see her. He waited around and talked to some of the employees until it was time for her to take a break.

Toni walks out into the lobby and sees Yusuf. She isn't too surprised, but she isn't very welcoming.

"Hey babe!" Said Yusuf. "You wanna have some coffee with me? You're on break now, right."

"Yeah, but I have some things to do."

"Well, can I speak to you for a minute outside?"

Toni walks out the door without answering and Yusuf follows.

"What do you want, Yusuf?"

"Are you really going to act like this because I went away? You know that this is childish, right?"

"Whatever! What do you want?"

"I miss you! I want to see you!"

Yusuf grabs Toni.

"I really miss you, babe." He says softly as he looks down at her and she's looking the other way.

Yusuf can't help but to laugh quietly to himself. He knows that she is furious with him, but he also knows that it's because she cares. They are still new and from what he knows about her so far, she hasn't actually been in a real relationship, so he understands (what he considers) her emotional immaturity. He just hopes that she comes around soon, because he really misses her.

Toni turns back to look up at Yusuf.

"I miss you too." She says with an emotionless face that says, 'I do miss you, but I don't want to."

Toni hugs him back and they kiss.

"Will you stop over tonight?"

"Okay. I'll be there."

Still no smiles from Toni, but Yusuf is elated and can't wait for this evening.

*Wine and Dine.*

Toni comes over to Yusuf's. He has the dining room table all set up with candles, with the lights dim and all of his finest china set out. He pulls out the chair for her to sit in. He then takes her plate to fill it with the gourmet dinner that he cooked for her. Italian chicken with New Orleans Spaghetti Bordelaise, asparagus sautéed in olive oil, and dinner rolls. He also had some prosecco for her to drink with dinner, because he knew that's what she liked. He finally got a smile from her.

"You're so corny!" Smirked Toni. She loved his attentiveness and the fact that he was trying to spoil her to get back on her good side.

"Yeah, maybe. But you're loving every minute of it."

Toni just looked at him with her mouth twisted hating that he was right.

"So, how was your trip?"

Yusuf wouldn't look her way because he felt like she was trying to start an argument, so he just answered.

"It was very productive."

Toni didn't really want to start a fight, so she accepted his answer then left it alone. They both just had some playful back and forth smack talk. Then they began throwing a lot of sexual inuendo at each other, until they both just wanted to go upstairs and have it out, sexually. The food and plates were just left on the table until Yusuf got up in the middle of the night to clean it up.

The next morning, they were back to normal and relieved that they were no longer at odds with each other. They overcame their first hurdle. Toni left out for work and Yusuf had some things to take care of following his trip.

----------

### *Servicing the Community.*

Yusuf had an eight-week course set up two nights a week for all in the community to attend a **Black Culture and History** class. He, and many other mentors, would discuss the history of Black people all around the world. Also, the cultural anthropological study of Black people. One of the most popular subjects was the Black Power movement. The parents of the children especially liked talking about it because most were a part of it in some way. It was a time of solidarity and pride.

The class became quite popular over the summer and many parents attended with their children. The churches and mosques encouraged attendance. Yusuf made it important to have relationships with all the religious clergy in the community. This was a time when religious differences were set aside.

Yusuf would give homework to the children and their parents. He would make each assignment so that it would inspire discussion between them. There would be an essay as a final assignment for each class and it would be a family event. All who lived in the same house would work on one essay.

The commencement of the class would be a trip to the National Museum of African American History and Culture in Washington DC for all of the attendees. It was a very popular trip, and for some, the reason for attending the class. Yusuf would have different community events throughout the year, to raise money for the trip.

He also had different professionals take teenagers and young men and women under their wings to teach them a **Trade**. All of these men volunteered their services out of an understanding of social responsibility and mentorship. He had most of the barbershop and beauty salon owners; electricians, carpenters and roofers; construction company owners and even retail store owners who took these young men and women under their tutelage to teach them a trade most of which they could use to make their own money for life.

This was a plan for young men and women to have a backup for being unemployed. This would hopefully prevent them from ever being in the system on public assistance; something Yusuf always hated for his people. Although he understood the need for financial help from time to time, he hated that many lived their entire lives dependent on a system that was intrusive, degrading, created poverty, separated families, and prevented the ability to save money. He wanted his people to learn to do for self and to help elevate each other without the help of the government.

There were also coding and IT programs that he was connected to and helped raise funding for. This was also another opportunity for the youth to create their own futures and to be able to work for themselves, whenever they were without a job.

There would be community meetings once a month to give the residents information about their **Rights as Residents** of any community and rights that were specific to their community. He would identify different public officials responsible for specific community issues and let them know the process of holding them accountable for their campaign promises.

Information was provided about the importance of making purchases within the community, and holding all stores and company's responsible for giving back to the community they are operating in. If a company is making money from the community residents, it's their social responsibility to give back to the community they are making money from. If they aren't helping the community in some way, the residents need to stop supporting them with their dollars. This was important to the **Economic Infrastructure** and growth of the community.

Another piece of the puzzle was to **Open Businesses** in their own community and for the residents to **Support Those Businesses**. This was a dual responsibility for the business owners and the residents. The business owners needed to be professional and customer service oriented, if they expected the community residents to patronize their businesses. And it was encouraged that they all have a suggestion box. Feedback would be one of the most helpful elements of running a business. It would also have to be accepted objectively and not taken personally.

Yusuf had **Self-defense** training classes set up for weekends. He had boxing and martial arts for children and adults. These were just training classes, no competition involved. He didn't want anyone, especially the children, being hit in the face and head unnecessarily. Learning skills didn't require beating on anyone to practice.

He also sponsored some of the older teens to learn how to safely and responsibly use, clean, maintain and **Shoot a Firearm**. This would be at the same range that he and Toni attended. This was controversial in the neighborhood, but those who did attend had the full approval of their parents. It was important to him that those in the community were able to always protect and defend themselves and to know their legal rights when it came to weapons rights and self-defense. People in other states were fully prepared to protect themselves and their properties to the full extent of the law. It was time for his people to be able to do the same.

# Sleeper

*Assassination.*

Toni and Yusuf are in bed asleep when Toni wakes up to a noise that sounds like a door unlocking; she's a light sleeper. She awakens Yusuf to tell him that she heard something. Yusuf isn't too concerned because his home has an alarm system and his rottweiler, Dagan, sleeps in the house. But he doesn't take anything lightly, so he reaches under the head of his mattress for his gun and two backup magazines, then slowly creeps out the bedroom, down the stairs.

He wonders where his dog is, but he takes his time and listens. He hears some movement towards the kitchen and slowly moves in that direction. He doesn't turn on any lights because he realizes that he will be in the spotlight; he also knows his home well, even in the dark. Yusuf sees a dark mass on the floor in the kitchen just a couple of feet from the entryway. As he approaches, the moonlight through the window gives him just enough light to tell that it is Dagan; he's motionless.

Yusuf falls back behind the entryway, knowing in his heart that Dagan is dead. His heart hurts from the pain of his buddy's demise, but he knows that he has to get his head together. He understands and realizes that something bad is going down and that he is the target. He again approaches the kitchen entryway, aware of Dagan's body on the floor, but using his senses to avoid it while stepping through and scanning the dark kitchen. A quick breeze passes the side of his face. He realizes that a bullet just missed him.

'A silencer! They mean business!' He thought.

He drops to the floor and behind the breakfast counter. He believes that the gunshot came from over by, or in, the kitchen cupboard. He peaks around the counter while on the floor to try to see if he could make out exactly where the gunshot came from, but he couldn't. He needed to decide quickly whether he wanted to unload a barrage of bullets on his kitchen cupboard, or if he wanted to wait for another movement or sound. He decided to wait.

He heard the cupboard door creek. He knew the sound well, so he stood up and emptied his clip, shooting at his kitchen cupboard. While he was shooting, he heard a gunshot in the living room, so he ducked back down behind the counter. It sounded like it was aimed towards the kitchen, but it didn't sound as if the bullet made it into the kitchen. It sounded as if it stopped at the entryway. He wasn't sure what just happened but heard a couple of thuds in the melee. He just sat quietly again to try and ascertain what just happened. He also pulled a second clip out of the back of the waistband of his boxers, to reload his gun.

There is a commotion happening in his living-room, and he is concerned that Toni might be in danger. So, he takes a chance to dart out of the kitchen, not knowing for sure if he hit his target or not. He trips on something outside the kitchen entryway and realizes that it's a lifeless body. Yusuf's heart sinks again.

'Toni!' He says her name silently in his head.

Yusuf remains silent as he swallows his fear, then uses his hand to identify her in the dark. He attempts to run his hand through her hair, but there is something covering it. It's a ski mask. Thank God it isn't Toni.

He remains on the floor and crawls towards the dining-room wall for cover from what is going on in the living-room. He doesn't hear Toni's voice or anything, so he's not sure what's happening in there. He's also concerned that he hasn't heard any sound from her at all.

He continues to hear some type of struggle and peaks around the wall to see what's happening. He can't really make it out at first, then he notices Toni with something wrapped around a person's neck. The person is still struggling and has a ski mask on, but Toni is in control and has a tight grip. The invader stops struggling, but Toni still holds on for about a minute more.

"Are you okay?" Whispers Yusuf.

"Yes, but I'm not yet positive that there aren't any more people around." Toni whispers.

Toni lets go of the lifeless body.

"I'm going to check outside to see what's going on out there."

"No!" Whispers Yusuf. "Let me do that!"

"Trust me!" Whispers Toni, "You want to let me do this."

Yusuf was baffled by her calmness and was thinking 'What woman attempts to walk into danger.' He wasn't sure what was going on but remained alert to the situation. He'd figure the rest out later when they were both safe. While Toni was checking outside, he checked the kitchen. He still didn't turn on any lights but wanted to see if he hit the person who was shooting at him from the cupboard. He had. The man was dead. Yusuf pulled out his phone and took a picture of the man's face.

After about five minutes, Toni came back in.

Still whispering, "The coast is clear! There's no car out there. Someone must've dropped them off. Probably planning to come pick them up, once they receive a phone call."

"Do you think there's anyone else in the house?" Yusuf didn't believe that there was but wanted to see what Toni would say.

"No! I don't, but one of us should check downstairs and the other, upstairs. And umm, I had an altercation in the bedroom, so there is a body in there."

Yusuf stared at Toni trying to understand her calm, what she just said, and what he saw a few minutes ago. He shook it off and went up the back stairwell from the kitchen. The three men that Toni encountered must've gotten upstairs this way. Toni checked the basement and it was clear. Once they felt they were safe, Yusuf made sure he took pictures of all the deceased; he then called the police.

When the police came, Yusuf explained what had happened. The police knew him well because of all his community activities; he had a good relationship with the police department. It looked to them like a home invasion gone bad. The bad guys lost. The entire home was a crime scene, so Toni and Yusuf had to go to a hotel. Yusuf left the keys to his home with the police captain with a promise to protect his home, and to call him when he was allowed to come back in.

He and Toni went to get a room at a nearby hotel. The police allowed them to put on some clothes, but they weren't allowed to touch much more. While at the hotel, Yusuf just kept staring at Toni trying to figure out who she really was. He didn't say much to her about his thoughts on her actions. Knowing how to shoot and fight were one thing; but knowing how to handle yourself and use those skills with the calm that Toni had, was another.

She knew he had questions, so she figured she'd just answer them without him having to question her. She sat on the bed next to him and made eye contact.

"Babe, I know that you have questions. So, I'm going to explain myself to you."

He remained quiet and looked her in the eyes.

"I have extensive self-defense training. My parents kept me in different types of martial arts and self-defense training classes and competitions. Also, I was in many firearm self-defense training classes, when I was growing up and for my job as a firearms instructor, too. That's why I was able to handle those men."

"Okay." Yusuf wasn't buying it, but he didn't want her to know.

"Just, okay?"

"I just had an assassination attempt on my life, Toni. I guess I'm a bit in shock."

"I can understand that, babe. I don't mean to add to your stress."

Yusuf wanted to be alone so that he could review the security files from his phone. He wanted to see every step that Toni took. He's no longer sure that she's an innocent in all this.

"Babe, if you need to go home and get some rest that's okay with me. I'm not going to be able to sleep and I need to make some phone calls."

"You sure you don't want to come with me? I know that it's a little hike, but at least you won't be in a hotel."

"No, I want to stay close so that I can get back home as soon as the bodies are cleared."

"I'm sorry about Dagan…"

"Yeah... me too..." Yusuf's heart was heavy as he thought about his rotty.

Yusuf drove Toni to his house so that she could get her car to drive home. He hugged and kissed her and told her that he would call when the police and coroner's office were done at the house. She said okay.

Once Yusuf got back to his hotel room, he jumped on his phone to view the security files to see what exactly happened. He couldn't see what happened in his bedroom because he didn't have a camera in there. He didn't want any accidental recordings of his bedroom activities. All he had was Toni's word on that, and he wasn't too sure about that anymore.

Yusuf made a phone call to his good friend, Mills, who was a police detective. He explained the happenings of the day and told him that he needed to find out everything that he could about Patrice Rice, nickname Toni. Once that was done, he called another friend, Jimmy, who owned a popular bar in the city. He knew everyone, or someone who knew whoever he didn't. He had a lot of connections and Yusuf asked him find out who these guys were who tried to kill him, and why? So, he sent him the pics of the dead men. He then called his brothers and told them what happened. They were on their way with a security team for his protection.

Yusuf's mind was all over the place. 'Who is trying to kill me? Who is Toni, really? Why is she so highly skilled in fighting? Why was she so calm during the assassination attempt? Why isn't she stressed about killing three people? Dagan is gone! I have too much to do today for all this.' His mind was frazzled a bit, but he knew that he had to hold it together.

There was a bang on the hotel room door.

"Open up! It's your brothers!"

His three brothers came with four, armed bodyguards. Two stayed outside and two remained inside. He told them everything that happened, but instead of wondering about Toni, they were very impressed with the story. Yusuf didn't tell them his concerns about her, because he wasn't sure himself. His instincts told him that it wasn't good, but he was full-fledged in love with her. There was too much going on for him to think straight, but he didn't want her to be around him until he received a full report on her that made sense.

### Antonaya Patrice Rice.

The background check on Toni came back –

Toni was born Antonaya Patrice Rice. She was the daughter of a college professor (her mother) and a senator (her father). Her parents were violently murdered during a home invasion at their home on the Main Line in Villanova PA, when she was 5 years old. She listened to the violent encounter from her bedroom closet. She was the first one to see their bloody battered bodies before she remembered what her parents taught her in case of an emergency, and that was to dial 911.

No family members could be located, so Toni ended up in the foster care system. And there she would stay for five years with no real counseling and therapy to try to counteract the traumatic experience. She would be verbally and physically abused in the system. She would be molested many times by foster brothers and friends and family of foster parents. She would go through hell for her five years following her parent's death.

Then her father's brother and his wife came forward to claim her. She had no idea that she had family. She would be raised by her aunt and uncle on her father's side. Her mother had no brothers or sisters, and her parents were elderly.

Toni finally received the therapy she needed and remained in therapy for years after her aunt and uncle took custody of her. They also wanted her to feel safe after all that she'd been through. So, they enrolled her in many different self-defense and martial arts classes through her childhood and teen years. And once she was old enough, they thought it would be a good idea for her to learn to shoot a variety of weapons. All of this would help her to regain a sense of power over her fears of being hurt again. And because of all she had been through, she excelled at all of it, since she had a reason to. She vowed that no one would ever hurt her again.

As he read the report, he realized that Mills dug deep to get such detailed information, and he was very grateful; he began to understand. Yusuf was now ready to see Toni, so he called her to come over. When she got there, he hugged her tightly.

"Thanks, so much babe! You saved my life, you know that, don't you?"

"No, babe! You saved us both. You were on it! I just helped where I could."

"Nah, but we're not going to fight over this... I really missed you."

"I really missed you too."

"I hope you understand that I couldn't let you come over until I found out who those killers were?"

Yusuf couldn't tell her that he was suspicious of her, so he told her part of the full truth.

"So, the killers were identified?" Said Toni.

"Yeah, they belonged to the drug gang that I told you about. The ones I had a run in with. I don't recognize any of them, but I found out that they do belong to the same gang. So, I'm not entirely safe until they can locate and arrest the rest of them. They are more likely than not, going to come after me again. And I got word today that you maybe a target too. They know that you killed a few of their guys, so maybe you should stay with me until they can arrest the leaders of the gang."

"Babe, I can take care of myself. I'm not going to live in fear. I refuse too."

"Toni, that means that I'll have to be on edge every time you're away from me."

"Well, I'm not altering my life because of those punks."

"Can you please just stay with me for a couple of weeks? Can you please just do that?"

"I'll think about it."

Yusuf just sighs out of frustration. He hopes that Toni changes her       mind       about       staying       with       him.

# Change

*Life Officially Altered.*

Toni chose not to stay with Yusuf. She felt it was safer for her to go home to where she lived in Delaware County. She remained alert to her surroundings. Yusuf was assured that an officer would be on duty at the range whenever she worked. Partially paid through his program and partially as a public service to the community.

Yusuf, however, stayed away from his normal community activities. He couldn't allow the children to be exposed to the danger he faced. He also wouldn't allow any of the adults to be put in danger. He needed an end to this threat, and soon.

With so much time on his hands, he decided to structure a plan to expand his program into other neighborhoods. He had many inquiries and hadn't had the time to spend to explain the details of such a huge undertaking. The program would be able to be implemented in any neighborhood that was interested. This would take time and he hoped that the rest of the gang would be caught by the time he finished it.

Yusuf didn't like being away from the kids and the programs, but he had qualified people in place to handle everything the way he would handle it. His mind was at ease on that front, it was just him missing the kids, and missing teaching and educating the community. His work was far from done. AND this was his purpose in life. He needed it as much as the air he breathed.

His brothers would stop by daily to check up on him and to spend time with him. He would cook for them and they would play cards like the old days. Sometimes he and his brother, Malik, would get a game of chess going. This helped to pass the time until the gang leaders were caught.

The highlight of his day would be when Toni stopped by. Today, two of his brothers would finally get to meet her. The third brother, Rasheen, couldn't make it today, but Yusuf introduced her to the other two, Malik and Haneef. It had been many years since Yusuf had been in a relationship, so they wanted to meet the woman who changed his status.

"Well, hello pretty lady!" Said Malik. "Now, what do you want with a big head negro like him? You could do so much better."

Everyone laughed.

"SHUT UP, Man!" Laughed Yusuf.

"We heard that you're some kind of super-hero," said Haneef. "They say that you took out a few bad guys. How did you get to be so brave?"

Toni nervously laughed. "Well, I'm no one's superhero. Our instinct for survival is our strongest instinct. I guess I just wanted to survive."

"Fair enough, but Malik would've just… ran the other way…"

"MANNN, BE QUIET! I'm not no punk!"

Everyone laughed.

"Rasheen couldn't make it tonight, so you'll have to meet him another day." Said Yusuf.

"Okay, cool!" Said Toni.

They all sat around talking. Toni got a kick out of the brothers telling about Yusuf's adventures growing up, then it started getting late and everyone was a bit tired, so his brothers finally left. This was Toni's night to stay over, so Yusuf couldn't wait for his brothers to finally leave.

He loved the nights that she stayed over, which would be about twice a week. The nights with her would keep his mind occupied and keep him in a happy state of mind. To stay occupied during the day, he continued to work on his community plan and also went to the range a couple days a week.

At the range, they were well aware of the danger Yusuf was in and assured him that they were all well covered. The gym that he attended always had a large amount of law enforcement officers who worked out there. His two bodyguards would be with him (he no longer felt he needed four), but the cops also had his back. This would keep him from being too cooped-up in his home.

One night, Toni is on her way home from Yusuf's house. She has some things to do in the morning. She doesn't want to fight the morning traffic trying to get home in time, so she decides to leave late that night.

Toni is on the highway driving south on I95 going home. There is hardly any traffic this time of night. She has her music on listening to some songs, then a song comes on that she can't stand. She starts changing the stations, going back and forth trying to find a station to listen to.

"Why is it that every-time a commercial is on one station, there's one on *every* station."

She lets out a big sigh when she notices a car is on the right side of her; it's not advancing. She looks over to see if it is someone she knows, trying to get her attention. It isn't. All of a sudden, she sees the passenger in the back seat, stick something out of the back, driver's side window. It's a gun! She practically floors her gas as her turbo drive boosts her speed quickly, while bullets began to hit her car.

As she's trying to outrun them, she feels a hot piercing pain in her arm.

"Shit! I'm hit!"

A bullet penetrates the back of her right arm, then exits the front of it, hitting and lodging into her dashboard. Toni knows that she has to gain control of the situation, or she will lose her life.

The car is hot on her tail, so she rapidly moves over to the right lane, then hits her brakes. She quickly ducks down until she falls back far enough to get behind them. As the car decelerates, she's pulling her gun from her holster, while bullets are hitting her driver's side window, passing through her car at several different points of exit. The front passenger is shooting at her too.

She then quickly moves back over right behind the car. She knows that she has three targets to hit in the car. She starts with the back-seat shooter, then the shooter in the front passenger seat. They both slump down with each intended shot.

The driver attempts to speed away erratically in an attempt to prevent his own demise. Toni shoots him in the right shoulder with expert precision, then allows him to advance away from her. She then shoots out both of his back tires. He loses control of the car and hits the right-side guardrail.

Toni pulls up behind the car. The airbag is deployed, and the driver looks unconscious. There is no movement. Toni doesn't take any chances. She has her gun out as she approaches the driver's side of the car. She begins to get a bit lightheaded and realizes that she is bleeding profusely from her arm. She's aware that she has to remain conscious.

She pulls the driver out onto the ground, then drags him behind the car. He begins to come to. Toni has her gun pointed at his face.

"Who are you? And why were those guys trying to kill me?"

"Bitch, call me an ambulance."

The driver can barely talk but decides to push back instead of complying to Toni's question.

"I'll call you an ambulance as soon as you answer my question."

"Fuck outta here!"

Toni shoots him in his left shoulder. He screams.

"Who sent y'all to kill me?"

Toni knows she doesn't have much time before she loses consciousness.

"FUCK YOU BITCH!!!"

Toni shoots the driver in the head. Walks back to her car, gets in, then passes out. When she awakens, she's in her own bed with her arm bandaged. She looks at the clock and realizes that she lost several hours from the time she lost consciousness, and the time the clock says it is. She calls the gun range to leave a message that she wouldn't be in today. She also texted the range's manager. She calls Yusuf but didn't want him to know about her ordeal.

"Hey babe! I'm not feeling too good today, so I'm just going to stay home and get some rest."

"Okay, babe! I hope that you feel better, but guess what?"

"What's up?"

"The leader of the gang who was trying to kill me and his underlings were found dead in the house they were living in. Also, three of their other members were found shot to death on 95 last night."

"WOW! Really? Who do they think did it?"

"Word is, another drug gang. It's sad and a shame that so many lives have been lost, but that's the nature of the beast. That lifestyle promotes and fans the flames of violence. I wish there could've been a different outcome."

"Well, at least your safe now, right?"

"Yeah… at least I'm safe." Yusuf confirms her statement with a bit of sadness in his voice.

Toni was unable to work for the rest of the week. She was able to hide her wound from Yusuf by claiming a pulled muscle and keeping her arm covered, even when they were intimate. He had no clue that she was the one who killed the three men on the highway.


### Back to Normal.

Yusuf was so happy to get back to his kids and the community activities. They all were happy to see him. He decided to throw a community party to celebrate the neighborhood, the accomplishments over the past couple of years and the residents who leaned into all of the programs he put in place to help the community become a decent place to live again.

He also wanted Toni to finally meet his family. She was hesitant, and not really ready, but she and Yusuf were closer than ever. The adversity of their lives being in danger, and the fact that they made it through pretty unscathed, deepened their bond and feelings for each other. Yusuf wanted his family to meet the superwoman who saved his life. At least, that's the story that he would tell.

Yusuf's parents had a family gathering just to welcome Toni. All his brothers were there along with his sister. A few cousins, aunts and uncles attended too. As Yusuf introduced Toni to his parents, his father was impressed with Yusuf's taste in his choice of a partner. He thought Toni was stylishly sharp and carried herself like a classy lady. He couldn't wait to engage in conversation with her to see where her head was at, but he couldn't help but tease her first.

"So, I hear that you're sort of a superhero! So, where's your cape? You look pretty normal to me. I know that I can take you." Yusuf's father couldn't help himself.

Toni laughs.

"I don't fight old men, sir. So, even though I wouldn't let you "Take" me, I could easily defend myself against an old man. Practically with my hands tied behind my back."

Everyone in listening range expressed a collective "Ooool…"

Then Yusuf's mother felt she needed to explain her husband.

"Toni, please don't pay any attention to my husband. He loves to antagonize people."

Toni laughed. "It's okay, Mrs. Halim. I've handled men like him before. Please forgive me if I send him back to you in tears, with his thumb in his mouth."

There was another collective "Ooool", then an "Oh damn, dad! I think you met your match." Yusuf's sister Ali was tickled by Toni's handling of her dad, who loved picking on people. She walked over to Toni to introduce herself. She held out her hand.

"I'm Ali, Yusuf's younger sister! Pleased to meet you, Toni!"

Toni grabs her hand to shake it and smiles as they make eye contact.

"Pleased to meet you too!"

Ali was a beauty, about 5'3" in height, dark-skinned, impeccable makeup, with beautiful locs that were dipped in light brown and blonde color. Her fitted clothing accentuated her petite figure, with her full hips and thighs, small waist and an ample bosom. Her bottom was perfectly round and sat out proudly as you viewed her from the side. Toni thought to herself,

'No wonder Black men love Black women so much. How can they not be in awe of such a powerful vision?'

Ali walked with a slow sexy stride that was sure to garner the attention of men and women alike.

"You have to excuse my dad! He loves to tease people. He's a really great guy, though." Ali chuckles.

"It's cool! I don't mind. I enjoy teasing back. I'm sure that he is a great guy. His son is an awesome man."

"I agree." Said Ali.

She and Toni stood and talked for a few minutes, then her mother called her.

Yusuf's brother, Rasheen, had been drinking too much as he usually did. He kept eyeing Toni. He then decided to approach her and ask her some questions, once his sister walked away.

"Where you from?"

"I grew up in Virginia."

"Where about?"

Yusuf decided to intervene.

"None of your business, man. Leave her alone."

Yusuf stands between Toni and Rasheen, facing Rasheen.

"I'm not bothering her," Rasheen leans to the side to get Toni's vindication that he wasn't bothering her, "Am I Miss?"

"No," said Toni.

"See? Now mind *your* business and let me get back to my conversation with the young lady."

"She *is* my business, now go bother someone else."

"Man, aint nobody bothering her. I'm just talking to her, now move outta the way."

Rasheen pushes Yusuf. Their other two brothers see the shove and decide to step in. They know that Yusuf hates when Rasheen starts drinking. They always get into it whenever he drinks.

"Yo Yo Yo!!! Come on now! Don't start tonight, y'all. We don't want Toni to think that we're a dysfunctional family, do we?" Says his brother Malik.

"He brings home some high saditty bitch and don't want nobody talkin' to her."

Yusuf goes after Rasheen for his disrespecting statement, but his brothers hold him back. Their father overhears his disparaging remarks.

"RASHEEN!!! GET OVER HERE!!!"

Yusuf's father pulls Rasheen to the side and has an obviously aggressive one-way conversation with him. Rasheen puts down his drink, then leaves. None of the siblings are ever disrespectful to their parents, Toni finds out from Yusuf that night. They were raised by parents who taught them the value and gift of parental protection, guidance and wisdom.

Toni would get to talk to all of his family members that night. She was quite impressed with their closeness and enjoyed the atmosphere of being within a tight knit family unit. Something that she never really had or experienced before.

## Chi-Town Moves

*Toni's In.*

Yusuf has to go away again for the fourth time since he and Toni have been together.

"Babe... I have to go to Chicago in a couple of days. I'd like you to go with me."

"WHAAATTT!?!? You want ME to go with YOU on one of your trips??? I'm flabbergasted!!!" Toni says sarcastically.

"Come on, can you go or not?"

"So, what's different this time?"

"Come with me and you'll find out."

"Okay, the answer is yes! I'll go."

"Cool! I'll make the reservations. We'll be staying from Thursday till Sunday, is that okay?"

"Yup! That's fine."

-------

Toni and Yusuf land at Chicago's O'Hare Airport. A shuttle takes them to the Enterprise car rental, where they pick up the Escalade that Yusuf reserved. They ride to the Hampton Inn on the Loop. They get to their room and unpack their luggage before heading out to their destination which is unbeknownst to Toni.

They arrive at a home in New City. It's an ordinary looking home in a rough neighborhood. A guy named Hassan answers the door.

"What's up man?"

"You, brother! How's it going?"

"It's all good, man. All good! And who do you have here, as if I have to ask?"

"This is my lady, Toni; Toni this is Hassan, a really good friend of mine and the family."

"Hello pretty lady! Pleased to meet you!"

Toni offers her hand. "Pleased to meet you too!"

"Naahh, nah nah nah... We don't greet family with a handshake, Ms. Lady. We hug, around these parts."

Hassan moves toward Toni to hug her as she hugs back. Yusuf begins to move into the room from the doorway as Hassan embraces Toni. Everyone gets up, happy to see Yusuf and greet him with a hug. He then introduces Toni to everyone. They all greet Toni with a warm embrace.

"So, you're the young lady that we have to thank for saving our man's life, huh?"

"I don't know about all that!" Toni says humbly.

"Yeah, well we know all about it. And we want to thank you for being there and being such a warrior. We respect and appreciate that kind of strength. Yus never did connect with ordinary women. And I'd say that you are quite extraordinary and perfect for my man. I'm happy he found somebody who can put up with his ass."

Everybody started laughing.

"Hey, hey, hey! Don't be trying to scare her away, now. Sheesh!"

They all laughed again.

Everyone sat around talking and eating and catching up. Then they all wanted to hear about how Toni killed the three men the night of the attempted assassination. Toni didn't want to talk about the incident, so Yusuf did it for her, with a few added liberties with the story. Toni would just look at him, stare, then shake her head when he embellished a few truths.

Hassan asked Toni how she became so good with self-defense, so she explained how her parents put her in self-defense classes most of her childhood and teenage years. Along with sending her to weapons training and competition for many years.

"I don't know if Yusuf told you why you were invited here." Said Hassan.

"No, he didn't!" Toni looked towards Yusuf with a "Why didn't you let me know" look. Yusuf just stared back and smiled at her.

"Well, Yusuf told us about your training and expertise. And we were hoping that you could train some of the ladies in our organization, self-defense and weapons use. We're a community organization similar to what Yusuf is doing in Philly. We would like to adopt his method out here in Chicago. Once our ladies are trained... Actually, I would like you to train some of our men too.

Then, I'm going to have them start training the teens self-defense and firearms usage."

"Wow! I appreciate the offer, but it will take some time for me to train everyone. I would have to stay in Chicago for a bit to do that. I have a job at home; and a life."

"Well, we are planning to make it worth your while. We'll triple your salary while you're here. I'm sure that your place of employment will take you back once the training is done. Yusuf also knows the people well and I don't think anyone would begrudge you a temporary leave of absence to triple your salary for a few months. If they do, I would reevaluate my place of employment."

"This is a lot, Hassan. This really caught me off guard. I need to think about all this and get back to you. Please understand that I am grateful and honored for the offer, it's just that I had no clue that this was going to happen. It's a lot to think about."

"Absolutely, Toni! I wouldn't expect anything less. Just give it some thought and let us know what your decision is."

"Okay, Hassan. Will do!"

"Alright! Well, let's just have a good time tonight, and tomorrow is another day."

So, they just played some card games and some chess while the music was playing in the background. Some people were just sitting and talking. Others were watching television. Most were drinking, and a few were smoking outside and talking.

They all had a good time that night.

The next day, Yusuf and Toni met Hassan and the rest of the crew at the house. They all rode to the community center that their organization worked out of. Hassan showed Toni around the center and explained the different offices and what they were for and who oversaw each office. She was quite impressed with it all. This was the part that Yusuf was still working on in Philly; to get a center up and running to the degree that Hassan had accomplished.

They then went to see another building that Hassan was trying to get to set up a center for teaching and training the kids. This was the part that Yusuf had already accomplished in Philly. It was the reason Yusuf kept traveling to Chicago, and also why Toni was invited. This would be where most of the training would happen, except for the firearms training. They had a local gun range where they wanted Toni to train the ladies to shoot. Everything else could be done at the center they were in the process of acquiring.

All of this gave Toni a lot to think about. After seeing the centers and having Hassan explain what they had already achieved and what was in the plans, Toni was really excited about it all. She wanted to say that she would do it on the spot but knew that she had to take care of things at home first. She couldn't wait to work it all out and get back to Chicago. Her only apparent hesitation was the fact that Yusuf wouldn't be with her. And she wasn't sure how often they would get to see each other while she was there.

"Baby, this is a great opportunity for you, and a wonderful opportunity to help the community here. It's greatly needed, and you will be able to say that you were a part of the solution. We'll work it out, and if worse comes to worse, when it's all over we will appreciate each other that much more."

Yusuf tried to give her the pep talk that she needed. He knew that this was part of a higher calling and would require him to pull away from the selfishness of his emotional needs. This, he knew how to do, well.

### Duty Calls.

Toni had made all the arrangements to take leave from her job and to stay in Chicago for at least six months to help train everyone. She was provided an apartment, free of charge, as part of the deal, and a loner car while she was there. The organization owned several apartment buildings in the area. Hers was fully furnished so she didn't have to worry about any of that. She just needed to go shopping for things like linens and curtains and bathroom towels. Just some things to personalize the apartment and to keep things at her level of sanitary.

She decorated the apartment to her comfort. She was quite satisfied with the finished project. Once she gave herself the thumbs up, she was able to relax and jump on her laptop to plan out her strategy to train the ladies and a few of the men. Half of the day was self-defense and the other half was weapons training. She would have a five-day work week with weekends off; and would see each person two to three days a week for training.

On the weekends, she would explore the Windy City. She would travel to the many historical sites and experience the famous foods that she'd always heard about.

Her first week there, Toni was missing Yusuf's cooking, so she asked around about soul food restaurants in the city.

She went to 5 Loaves Eatery on East 75th St. She ordered the fried chicken with some greens and macaroni and cheese, candied yams and potato salad. She couldn't even eat it all and took half of it home. It wasn't quite like Yusuf's, but it was delicious none the less. She would have something to snack on through the night and maybe even some for the next day.

During her stay, she would visit Daley's Restaurant, Fat Johnnies, Leon's Barbecue and several more local restaurants, when she didn't feel like cooking herself.

She would visit the William Rainey Harper Memorial Library and was in awe of its beautiful architecture. She stopped by the Wood Street Urban Farm to check it out. She heard Hassan and his crew talk about how they buy as much as they can from Green City and Logan Square Markets, because they sell produce that comes from the Urban Farm, which has a community-based foundation.

She wondered if Yusuf had ever visited the farm. She would suggest it to him when they talked again. They needed something like that in Philly.

She would check out the Riverwalk, their Chinatown section, and rode by the Ida B Wells-Barnett House, which actually sits on Martin Luther King Drive. She felt reverence for the history as she drove by the house and on the drive named after Dr. Martin Luther King, Jr. She wished that she was able to go into the house, but it is now a private residence; although it is designated as a national landmark.

-------

Toni and Hassan had a business dinner to discuss how the training was going. Hassan was pleased with the progress of everything and thanked Toni for all her help and sacrifice. The conversation shifted to personal questions out of Hassan's curiosity about Toni. He ended up asking her how she and Yusuf met, so she told him the story.

"Are you in love with him?" Said Hassan.

The question caught Toni off guard.

"What!? Why?"

"I have a reason for asking."

"Well, I haven't really thought about it."

"It's just that I really dig you. Yusuf is my boy and all, but if you guys aren't together, together… well…"

"Well, we are together, together. And I think it's fucked up that you're trying to make a move on me."

"Look! I apologize! Please don't let this affect our plans. I just wanted to know, that's all."

"All this is bigger than us both, so no… it's not going to affect our agreement. But I *am* going to leave to go home. Thank you for dinner."

Toni got up to leave and Hassan just sat there feeling like an ass for just making a move on his friend's girl. He wasn't very proud of himself, but he also couldn't get Toni off his mind. He felt he needed to reconnect with his own integrity, to find the words to talk himself out of the disloyalty of having feelings for his friend's girl. If he couldn't do that, he had to find a way to distance himself from her while she was in Chi-town.

As soon as Toni jumped in her car, she received a call from Yusuf.

"Hey babe! Whatchu up to?"

"Hi babe! Just leaving a business dinner with Hassan."

"Cool! How'd it go?"

"All is well! He wanted to let me know how pleased he is with how things are going. And thanked me for my help."

Toni didn't want to get between their friendship, so she didn't tell Yusuf about the conversation that transpired between Hassan and herself.

"Great! What are you about to do now?"

"I'm on my way to the apartment to get some rest."

"Okay, give me a call once you get settled."

"Okay, babe!"

Once Toni got to the apartment, she was getting ready to get undressed to jump in the shower. There was a knock on her door. She hoped it wasn't Hassan. She peeped through the peephole but couldn't see anything.

"Who is it?" She shouted with an attitude.

"Open the door, woman!"

It sounded like Yusuf. She couldn't wait to get the door open. When she did, she saw Yusuf to the right of the doorway and was happy to see him.

"You play to damn much! That's how mo' fo's get shot."

She grabbed him, and they hugged and kissed before Yusuf came into her apartment. Once he stepped inside, he looked around and was impressed with the place.

"Okay, I see they treatin' you good. This is nice, babe!"

"Yeah, I like it too. What are you doing here? You could've let me know that you were coming. I really miss you babe!"

"Yeah, I could've but I wanted to surprise you."

"Well, this is a nice surprise. How long are you staying?"

"Just for a few days."

"Well, are you here for me or for the organization?"

Yusuf looked at Toni. "Does it matter?"

"Yeah! I want to know if you came just to see me, or not."

"Come on girl, *stop it*!"

"So, you came for the organization. That's cool! I'm still happy to see you, either way; so, what's going on?"

"Hassan just has to show me a few things and we also have some stuff to talk about."

"Okay, so where're you staying?"

Yusuf turned towards Toni, stared at her for a few seconds, then laughed, "Haaaa, your funny!"

Toni started laughing. She knew that he wasn't going to be staying anywhere but with her. She couldn't resist teasing him.

"Where're your things?"

"They're in the trunk of the car. I'll get them out later. I couldn't wait to see you."

They started kissing.

"I need a shower, baby." Said Toni.

"Okay, I'll join you."

They took a shower together and it ended up being an intense lovemaking session. They really missed each other and made up for it three times that night.

Toni decided not to join Yusuf while he was with Hassan. She always made excuses that she had other things to do. She would see him when they met at her apartment. After Yusuf's time was up in Chicago, Toni hated to see him go, but he had to go back to Philly to implement some of the things that Hassan had shown him.

Toni and Hassan managed to keep their distance from each other for a while, until one of the young ladies she was training had a birthday party. She pleaded with Toni to make sure that she made it, so Toni didn't want to disappoint her. It was to be a semi-formal event in red, black and white.

The night of the party, Toni wore the red dress she bought specifically for the party; she knew that red was her color. When she walked into the room, heads turned because no one had ever seen Toni dressed up. She looked stunning like a model with her perfect curvy figure and her above average height; especially with her heels on.

Hassan couldn't take his eyes off her and needed to finally break the ice. He walked over towards her but didn't want to get too close.

"You weren't supposed to outdo the birthday girl." He softly spoke to Toni from the side.

She looked over to see that it was Hassan. She couldn't help but to look him up and down and think to herself how handsome a man he was. He cleaned up really well, but she kept that in her head.

"I'm sure that I haven't." Toni said as if he didn't move her, but he did.

"How are you making out, outside of work; you missing home?"

"Somewhat, but my focus is on getting things completed here, so there's no real time to miss home. I'm also appreciating the Chicago experience. It's a nice city, in spite of its recent reputation."

"Yeah, well, the news media always spins the negative over the positive. Which almost always outweighs the negative. They show all of the killings here but neglect to show how many of us are providing solutions. It's going to take some time to take the streets back, but the plan is in place and being implemented. But we also don't want our plans broadcasted either."

"I understand and agree."

Everything got quiet between them for the next few minutes, then Hassan decided to break the silence.

"I'm truly sorry for attempting to make a move on you and I want to apologize again. I respect you and I respect Yusuf, and now I respect your relationship."

"Thank you." Toni wanted to keep it short. She felt that the apology was genuine and didn't want the tension to linger. She and Hassan continued their conversation about the community and plans to help turn it around.

Toni stayed at the party for about an hour or so; just long enough to make an appearance and to say happy birthday to the birthday girl. She then left to go back to her apartment.

# Wait!?! What?!?

*Training Complete.*

Today would make Toni's fifth month in Chicago. She had one more month before she would be headed back to Philly. Toni was finishing up training all of her students. During today's training session, there was a major delivery happening. In between training sessions, Toni inquired with one of the guys about what was being delivered. He just told her that he didn't know and that his job was to just get it into the room. Toni didn't believe him.

Another one of the guys, Tarik, overheard Toni asking questions.

"You need to mind your business!"

Toni always got the feeling that he didn't like her.

"So, what is your problem with me? I see the way that you look at me. It's obvious that you don't like me, but what did I ever do to you?"

"I just don't like you and whatever my reasons are is my mother fucking business."

"I agree with that! But my questions were for him, not you, so you need to mind *your* mother fucking business!"

"You uppity bitch! Don't think that I won't fuck your ass up! You aint the only one who can fight. And since your so bad, I don't have a problem fucking you up! Even though you're just a *bitch*."

Toni was well warmed up for a fight and it had been a while since she had an actual opponent.

"Put your money where your mouth is, PUSSY!"

Those words set Tarik off in a bad way, so he took a fighting stance with Toni. She wasn't sure which technique he was about to use, so she made an advance to see his defensive moves. He was using Krav Maga. She knew she had to be careful, but also knew how to handle him. She just didn't know yet how good he was.

As they started to fight, some of the class members were trying to break it up, while others were attempting to call Hassan. The guys bringing in the delivery were ordered to continue until finished, so they didn't get involved. This was an important and classified delivery for the organization, and it needed to be quick and smooth.

Toni assured the students that she could handle Tarik and not to worry. Hassan was calling Toni's phone and Tarik's phone to no avail, because they were in the midst of fighting. He stopped calling, then dropped what he was doing to get to the Center. When he got to the Center, the fight was over, and Tarik's nose was bloody, while Toni had a few bruises.

"What the fuck is going on?" Said Hassan.

"I told this nosey bitch to mind her business!" Said Tarik.

"Wait a minute! Apologize to the lady! You don't get to call her a bitch, man!"

"I'm not apologizing to nobody!"

"Yo! Get the fuck outta here, man! I'mma talk to you later."

Tarik left as Hassan apologized to Toni.

"That's not your job, Hassan. And fuck him. All I did was ask a question. And it wasn't even to him."

"Well, I'm still apologizing because he's a part of my crew. Are you alright? Did you need to cancel class for the day?"

"Absolutely not!"

"Alright then."

Hassan went to check on the shipment to make sure that all was well.

When the workday was done, Toni hung around until mostly everyone was gone. She was curious about the shipment that came in today. When the coast was clear, she went over to the door of the room where the shipment was dropped and pulled on the door. It was locked, as she expected.

Toni looked around to make sure that no one was looking, and she also knew that the internal video surveillance system was not yet in place. She used her skills to open the lock without a key. She quickly went into the room and closed the door. Once again, she used her skills to pry open one of the containers. They contained AR15's.

Toni stayed in the room and locked it from the inside because she knew that the door would be checked before everyone left. Once she knew that everyone was gone, she had to get to the alarm panel to disarm the system so that the motion detectors didn't set the alarm off, while she was moving around. She disarmed it, then a call came in from the monitoring station to make sure that there weren't any unauthorized personnel there after hours. The security rep asked for her code, she gave them one.

"Thank you, Ms. Halston!" The rep was satisfied with the code.

The code Toni used belonged to one of the centers managers. Now Toni was able to wander around without worrying about being caught. She checked all of the cases that had been delivered that day. There were 100's of illegal weapons in the cases.

She then went into the office to check the external video recordings. Even though they hadn't installed the internal recorders, the external ones were already in place. She needed to get the license plates of the trucks that delivered the weapons.

She made a phone call to report her findings, then put everything back the way she found it, reset the alarm system, then left. She made sure that she parked out of the range of the building and its external camera's so that it wouldn't be noticeable that her car was still there after hours. Although, she disabled the recorders so that she wouldn't be recorded leaving the premises.

The next day, a caravan of FBI and ATF agents surrounded and entered the building. They gathered everyone who was in the building, including Toni, and kept them contained. They asked for someone to open the room that the shipment was locked in. No one claimed to have the key, so the agents kicked the door in.

They found all the illegal weapons, so everyone was arrested. Many of those who were a part of the organization was on a watch list, so once the weapons were identified, all of those members were arrested, simultaneously.

Once everyone was booked, only a couple were let go on their own recognizance,

including Toni. When she got to her apartment, she began packing to go home. She gathered what she needed, then was ready to catch her flight to Philly, when there was a bang on the door.

"Shit!" Toni needed another way out. There was no back way out of her apartment. The only thing she could think of was the bedroom window. She grabbed her bags and went to peak out of the window to see if the coast was clear.

"Toni! Open the door! We need to talk to you!"

It sounded like Tarik. She knew that he wasn't coming to talk. And she knew that he wasn't alone, for a reason. So, Toni lifted the bedroom window and threw her bags out. She was on the first floor, so her jump wasn't too bad. She gathers her bags, then two people come from both sides of the building.

"Leaving so soon, bitch?" Tarik grabbed Toni's arm and she instinctively hit him. Tarik and the other three men began to fight Toni, and she was getting the best of them all, even though they were getting in a few good hits here and there. Eventually, Tarik pulled out a gun.

"Bitch! If you don't stop right now, I will gladly blow your motherfucking *rat* brains out."

Toni, stopped, because she knew that he would do it. And she wasn't in a good position to knock or take the gun out of his hands. One of the guys used a plastic zip tie to bind her hands. They threw her in back of the enclosed F-350 truck with tinted windows, then bound her feet with zip ties, too.

"Well, waddu we have here?" Said Melvin.

"What is it?" Asked Tarik.

"She had a knife strapped to her ankle."

"Search her for any more weapons, then find her phone and throw it out the window; and use your gloves." Said Tarik.

"You sure man? We may be able to get some information from the phone." Said Melvin.

"Nah, we know what the fuck she is; we just don't know who she is, yet. Besides, these phones have GPS's on them now. We don't need anyone following us to where we're taking her. I don't know what type of organization she may be connected to; or if she's just a plain ole *rat*."

Melvin searched her and found a gun in a custom holster in the crevice of her back and waist. He removed both the holster and the gun. He also found her phone and tossed it out the window.

"Found a gun; and tossed her phone."

"Okay, hold onto the gun."

Toni wasn't saying anything. She was deep in thought trying to figure out how to get out of the situation.

------------

When Toni landed at Philly International Airport, she got a taxi to take her directly to Yusuf's. When he opened the door, he was surprised but happy to see her.

"What are you doing here, babe?"

Yusuf grabbed and hugged Toni, happy to see her.

"We have to talk." She said to Yusuf.

"What's going on babe?"

"Let's talk inside."

"Yeah, of course."

He and Toni went inside to the living room.

"Have a seat."

"No, Yusuf. I can't stay long."

Yusuf noticed the serious and stressed look on Toni's face. It made him nervous.

"Tell me what's going on." Said Yusuf.

"Hassan and his organization have been arrested."

"Whoa! What do you mean?"

"They have been arrested for illegal weapons possession."

"WHAT? So, what are you doing here? Why didn't you call me from there?"

"Yusuf…" Toni hesitated, but knew she had to come clean.

"I'm an intelligence agent. We have been after Hassan's organization for some time."

"Wait, wait, wait… Hold on… You're WHAT???"

"I'm sorry!"

"Hold on. I need to wrap my head around this. So, am I a target? Did you use me to get to Hassan?"

"Yes… You were used to get to Hassan."

Yusuf couldn't believe what he was hearing. He stared at Toni.

"So, you just used me. We were never really a couple, right?"

"Right." Toni looked Yusuf in the eyes while she told him the painful truth.

Yusuf wasn't sure if she was there to arrest him too.

"What the fuck do you want here? Are you going to arrest me?" Yusuf was angry and confused and wasn't sure if agents were outside waiting for his arrest.

"No. At least not yet, but they may try to tie you into the ring."

Yusuf couldn't believe what he was hearing.

"Okay, then get the fuck outta my house, and outta my life, you fucking traitor."

Toni left, knowing that Yusuf would be in pain about her and about his unintentional part in the arrest of his friends. She jumped into the back of a black car with tinted windows.

Yusuf called Chicago to get in touch with whoever he could. He also booked a flight to Chicago for as quickly as he could. Once he got to Chicago, he found out which jail Hassan was being held in, but he was unable to see him. He got in contact with one of Hassan's brothers who told him all that he knew, which wasn't much.

His brother then got Yusuf a meeting with Hassan's lawyer. Once he got to the lawyer's office, he told Yusuf about the raid, but wouldn't elaborate on the weapons that were found. He also told Yusuf about Tarik and five of his boys being ambushed and killed on the road. Yusuf could hardly believe what he was hearing. He stayed in Chicago to try to help in any way he could.

# Spy

*The Assignment.*

About a year prior, Toni was briefed on what was named as a Black Identity Extremist organization run by Yusuf Halim, in order to infiltrate the organization, to get to a brother organization in Chicago. The Chicago organization had ties to an international gun ring, and intelligence needed to identify the operatives that were on U.S. soil. They needed Yusuf in order to get Toni into the Chicago organization. This would be the break they needed to confiscate the weapons and to identify the U.S. link to the gun ring.

The background that Toni was given, was that Yusuf grew up with parents who were Black Nationalists. He grew up being taught that Black people needed to stick together, because this country was not going to allow Blacks to advance any more than they wanted them too. They needed their own; their own businesses, their own schools, their own banks, their own grocery stores... they needed to truly and completely own their communities in order to have a fair advantage in a country that put roadblocks before them, every step of the way.

They also needed to form their own special forces to protect them from the powers that be. Toni's bosses made it clear that the Halim organization was training and arming themselves to fight against the government authorities who would try to come and interfere with their community; and they knew that it was inevitable.

The FBI was already watching Yusuf, so none of that was Toni's concern. Her concern was to get an "in" with the Chicago organization who was dealing with arms from an international ring. The information from the FBI allowed the CIA to target Yusuf to get to the Chicago organization.

What Toni learned the real truth to be, by spending so much time with Yusuf, was that his parents were former Black Nationalists, so he grew up in a family that taught Black history and Black pride at home. He had heard all the stories of racism and slavery, and also the stories of African kings and queens. Along with the knowledge that human life started with the Black man being the original man and that all of humanity started with him/her.

Nothing and no one could make him feel less pride in his people. He didn't believe in labels and wasn't affiliated with any specific groups, but he did study many religions, philosophies and ideologies, and considered himself a free thinker.

He could never shake the feeling that his people needed to unite and have their own communities, schools, farms, gardens, stores, etc. From the time that he was a little boy, he wanted to learn self-protection, and was always respectful and helpful to the elderly. He was always a gentleman to women, even those who didn't appreciate his chivalry. He believed that all women should be treated with love and respect, even the mean ones.

Toni realized that the agencies understanding was twisted on who Yusuf was, and she needed to find a way to get that point across, to protect Yusuf. She had fallen for the man she used to get to her target. She felt compelled to protect him, the man she was sent to use as a pawn in the game of espionage.

*The Setup.*

Toni's assignment was to become an instructor at the gun range that Yusuf practiced at. She was already a marksman and had become a weapons expert with every street weapon the drug boys and street gangs were known to possess. Toni could hit a bullseye over and over as many times as she would shoot, at any distance the ammunition was capable of traveling. She could also take apart and clean every weapon she was able to use, as if it were a part of her own body. There was nothing that anyone could tell her about any of those weapons.

She had become skilled in many of the martial arts with Krav Maga being the one she chose to master. She would use all of this, so that she could impress and have an in, with Yusuf, who had no interest in average or ordinary women. He loved strong independent women who could give him a run for his money, and who could match his intelligence and wit.

Toni was all of that and more. She had an afro-centric look with natural twists in her hair, and the body of a goddess; curvy and fit. She's of high intelligence and has her master's in psychology and in information technology. She speaks seven languages fluently and she's also studied the history of Black Nationalism and the new term that was being used, Black Extremist, in order to step into this assignment. She had to understand the mindset.

But what happened instead, was that Toni got to know Yusuf, his organization, his vision for his people and community. He helped to educate her about the Black culture and what it meant to be a part of that community. He wasn't anti White and anti-establishment like she was led to believe. He was pro-Black and for his people and their advancement.

He didn't believe it could happen without being self-sufficient and doing for self. He had no interest in depending on a government that had shown their racisms and implicit biases against people of color. He wasn't interested in continuing the attempt to educate the ignorant. To him, it was time to take care of his own and teach them how to take care of themselves.

*The Result.*

Toni began to feel that she needed to find a way to help and protect Yusuf, even though she knew he hated her guts, at this point. She understood and deeply believed in his mission. He could become collateral damage in a world game that was much bigger than him; and she felt that that would be a travesty. He was the answer to what all communities should realize. And he could lose it all because of his connections to the Chicago crew.

She also felt that even *they* were doing the right thing but got caught up because they chose to use the illegal gun trade to fund a good cause. Their choices put them in the bad place they ended up in, albeit for the right reasons. She couldn't fight their fight, because it would be a fight against the oath she took to protect and serve the United States. It would be against everything that she stood for as an agent.

But she knew in her heart that Yusuf wasn't a part of the selling of weapons. And he wasn't against the US. He is just a man who's passionate about and for his people. He would be her focus and her fight, and she knew in her heart that it wouldn't be against the oath she took.

### What's Next?

Toni knew that she needed to talk to Tom to find out what her next assignment would be. She walks into his office to have a meeting with him about it. She takes a seat in the leather tufted chair as she waits for Tom to finish his phone call. She looks around as if she'd never been in there before, because she normally doesn't have to wait for their conversation to start. She notices many books on bookshelves, and his awards, degrees and certifications. He finishes his phone call…

"Good morning Antonaya!"

"Toni, sir. Good morning! What's next for me?"

"Well, you need to be debriefed and then we need you to lay low for a while. Take a vacation. Enjoy yourself. We will have your next assignment within the next few weeks… Good job on your last assignment!"

"Thank you, sir."

"We'll be in touch."

Toni needed to find out what was going to happen to Yusuf, but she couldn't let on that she had feelings for him. She was concerned that her organization might try to pull him into the gun ring case, but she was sure that he had nothing to do with it, and no prior knowledge of it.

"Sir?'

"Yes, Antonaya!"

"Toni, sir! What's going to happen to Yusuf Halim?"

"Why? That's none of your concern."

She knew that she had to be careful, but Tom began to suspect that she may have feelings for him.

"I know, but he's one of the good guys and I was just wondering if he was going to be caught up in the gun ring case?"

Tom looked at Toni and stared for a few seconds.

"Have you fallen for this guy? You know that's against everything that you're taught. He's off limits to your feelings. You are an agent of the United States government, Antonaya. Act like it!"

"No, sir! No feelings here! I was just curious."

"Okay! Well, lose your curiosity. He's not your concern. Go take that trip and get your head ready for your next assignment."

Tom practically barked at her, so she knew that it was time for her to leave. She didn't need him to have any more suspicions of her having feelings for Yusuf.

# Who IS Toni Rice?

*The Truth.*

Once Toni was debriefed and had time to actually relax, she began to think about all that she learned about Black culture. Then she realized that she didn't really know a lot about her mother. She was raised by her father's brother and his wife, who was of mixed ethnicity (Black and White). And she never discussed anything about her Black culture.

Toni contacted her mentor, Shomely, who was now retired. Someone who she became close to and who she cared about. She told him how spending time with Yusuf opened her eyes to so much about her mother's culture; Black culture. Even though her father was White, she never felt like she belonged in her White world, because of how she looked; she didn't look White. She wanted to know the full story of her background, her father's background and her mother's background. Shomely felt it was time to tell her the truth about what really happened to her parents.

Word was that they were targeted for assassination. On record, it was claimed that a Black Nationalist organization killed her parents, but that wasn't the truth; although he was unable to tell her who did kill her parents. He believed that is was someone in the very organization that they worked for, but he couldn't prove it, nor was it his place.

He told her that she was intentionally left in the foster care system. It was known that the families that she was left with were pieces of shit, but they (the organization or someone in the organization) wanted her damaged. The abuse and pain that would be inflicted on her would make her stronger. And would make her perfect for an agent.

"Was the abuse ordered?" Toni was hurt by the truth.

"I really don't know. It's certainly possible, but I don't know, Toni." Shomely felt for Toni, but also wanted her to finally know all that he came to know about her situation.

The people who raised her, were not really her family. They were planted as another means to create her into the perfect agent. They were told to feed her all the negative information they could about Black Nationalism. They were also commanded to strongly encourage her to work for the Intelligence Agency and to become a spy. They did their job well. These people had PHD's in psychology. They were married as a cover for their job in the Intelligence Agency.

"Why were my parents targeted? Why go through so much to make **ME** into a spy? I don't understand! This seems to be personal in some way."

Toni was right! It was personal, but Shomely never knew the complete story of why this all happened. He couldn't give her the answers to those questions and didn't know who could other than her boss, Tom. And Shomely told her to tread carefully if she decided to ask him for information. Toni wasn't sure where she was going to go from here, but she knew that she would never stop until she found out why her parents were targeted.

Shomely cared about Toni and always seemed to say things to her to let her know to trust no one and to always protect herself. He taught her to think objectively when it came to the agency. To always know that she is expendable and to keep some type of trump card that may save her life one day. This became top of mind to Toni as she would embark on her journey to find out why her parents were really murdered.

### The Why.

Toni needed to find a way into Tom's office. She needed access to his files but knew that it would be close to impossible for her to get past his security codes. She thought of another way into his files; an inside hacker who she was tight with. Someone who was secretly in love with her and would do almost anything for her. Lizbeth Ryan loved Toni from afar. They were close friends at one time, but Liz knew that she had to create distance between them, or it could be a bad situation for them both. Toni knew that Liz was in love with her but chose not to acknowledge it.

Liz was one of the top hackers for Tom. He trusted her with a lot of sensitive information. Her integrity was impeccable. But when Toni told her what she found out, Liz was furious and agreed to help Toni find answers. She had the clearances needed to get to her boss's files. She would scan them for the information that Toni needed. She would not divulge anything else she came across.

It took Liz several months before she would come across any of the information that Toni needed, but it wasn't in Tom's file; it was in another operations officers file. A peer of Toms. She thought twice about letting Toni read it, but she really wanted to help her friend. She used a flash drive to copy the information. Toni would only see the information Liz felt she needed to see, so that she maintained the integrity of the security. All other information remained secured.

As Toni read the file; which contained copies of notes, emails and transcripts of recordings, too; she found out that Tom and her mother were lovers for many years, until her father came along. It was a clandestine love affair because of Tom's job. Even though he was no longer in the field, he still didn't want the burden of a love interest or family. It would be too risky for him and too risky for them.

He was deeply in love with Toni's mother, but her mother wanted more than the secret lifestyle she had to live with Tom. She knew and understood why it had to be secret. That's why it lasted for two years, but two years was enough for her mother. And she had met this amazing guy, a senator, who wanted to be her everything.

So, she ended up marrying the senator. Tom tried to accept her decision and became involved with several other women, but Charlene touched him in ways that no one else could. He became almost obsessed with trying to get her to be a part of his life again. He didn't care that she was married to someone else. That would actually be the perfect cover for him and her, but she wanted no parts of it. She was head over heels in love with the perfect man for her. And he, Jordan, felt the same about her.

One day, Tom convinced her to meet him at his office that was a front. He had a private law office that he would use whenever he didn't have to be at the intelligence office. She agreed to meet him there. When she got there, he told her that he wanted her to still be a part of his life, even if he could only see her once in a while. She told him no. Everything about her at that moment; from her beauty, her style, her hair, her perfume, her heels; overwhelmed him with emotion and the desire to be inside of her, so he grabbed her and forced himself on her.

No one could hear her screams because he intentionally had the office sound proofed because of his position. When he was finished, he attempted to apologize but she just pulled herself together and left. She felt foolish for ever going to his office, so she never spoke of the rape to anyone, until she could no longer live with the emotional pain of what he did to her.

It took Charlene several years and a lot of therapy, but she finally told her husband what had happened and about her history with Tom. Jordan was furious. He went to confront Tom, but that was a mistake. Although Tom wasn't in the field anymore, he continued his self-defense practice at least three times a week. Jordan went to his law office front to face him about the rape and they got into a brawl. It was a quick fight with Jordan leaving with a broken nose.

Tom knew that Jordan was a U.S. senator and could cause him problems. He made sure that he was never able to get the chance. That same night is when Charlene and Jordan were massacred in their own home. It was the same night that the creation of a top spy began.

Toni was truly the product of a plot to destroy her parents and to destroy any purity that she might have grown up with. How deep must his hate be to intentionally destroy a child's innocence? She wondered how much hate he really had for her, and when would he sacrifice her for the cause?

Toni was sickened as she read the information, but what could she do? The agency obviously knew about it, it was in a buried file. Why wasn't he reprimanded? Why wasn't he fired? There were still a lot of unanswered questions.

Toni had to find a way to hold something over Tom's head in order to preserve her own life and safety. Would she have to kill him? She wondered. And would she be able to get to him? She knew that she could, but she also knew that she would probably lose her life in the process, or in the least, be on the run for the rest of her life. She needed to figure this all out.

*Hacker.*

Toni enlisted Liz to get every bit of information on Tom that she could. She would use all the info Liz would uncover to come up with a plan to keep herself safe. Toni told her to use all precautions to protect herself and to not do anything that could cost her, her life. Liz knew what business they were in, and they both knew that death could be the end result of being an agent; even though Liz was on the information side of the game and not in the field. Her job was a bit safer, but not safe by any means.

Toni decided to play the game and go on vacation. She chose to go to Barcelona, Spain. She had a rich Spanish lover who lived there. She gave him a heads up that she would be coming, so he had a suite prepared for her at his hotel.

Before she left, she needed to talk to Yusuf. She wasn't sure how to contact or meet him because she believed that she might have been being watched. 'Think Toni! Think, think, think…' Toni thought hard about how she would contact Yusuf.

She decided to buy a burner phone so that her call couldn't be traced. She used one to call a young lady who she befriended and was a friend of Yusuf's. She texted her and asked her to meet her. Her name was Kelly, but she and Toni had nicknames for each other, so Toni ended her text with the nickname Kelly gave her, "Sugar Tresses." She gave her that name because she loved Toni's beautiful hair and she told her that her coils were the color of brown sugar.

Kelly met Toni at a diner that they went to once. They hugged, and Toni couldn't tell her much, only that she needed Yusuf to meet her at a certain coffee shop and when. Kelly wanted to know what happened between her and Yusuf, but Toni apologized for not being able to explain and pleaded with her to get the message to Yusuf to meet her.

Kelly did get the message to Yusuf and he did meet her at the coffee shop. Toni was already there waiting for him when he arrived. He stared at her for about a minute before he walked to her table. She seemed to be sitting there watching the TV up on the wall, but she was deep in thought with her eyes just fixated on the television.

He missed who he thought she was and her perfect company, although it was all an act. Then he came to his senses and remembered that she was the enemy. But that didn't stop his feelings and that was the reason why he even showed up to meet her.

"What do you want Toni?"

Toni looked up to see that it was Yusuf. She wasn't sure if he'd show up. She stood up to hug him, but he sat down so that she couldn't.

"I need to explain myself and to let you know that you still have to be careful"

"Explain yourself?" Yusuf let's out a single chuckle.

"What's there to explain? You're a lousy two-faced spy. The worst of our people. You infiltrated an organization that's trying to get our people to understand who they are and where they came from, so that we can get back to being, a prideful, organized, and prosperous culture. Something that the people you work for took from us."

Toni allowed him his anger at her. She let him express his disdain for her without interference no matter how much it hurt.

"Yusuf, I know that nothing that I say can change how you feel about me, but I want you to know that you have to be careful. They may try to pull you into the case in Chicago."

"I WONDER WHY?" Yusuf raised his voice at Toni's audacity. In his mind, she was the reason why he may be pulled into the Chicago case.

"I'm risking my career to come here and tell you this?"

"For what reason, Toni? Why don't you explain that to me? Why would you do such a thing?"

"Will you please let me explain and say all that I need to without interruption? Then I will walk out of your life forever."

"Bet! Say what you need to say, then **SCRAM**!"

Toni wanted so bad to respond to his shitty remark, but she needed to get what she had to say out without an argument, hopefully. So, she just ignored his insulting response.

"Yusuf, no matter what you think or believe about me, I'm sorry for what I did to you. It was my assignment and I had no idea that I would have an education about my culture that I never knew about. You're not the person that was described to me. Your organization is not the group they have portrayed it to be. Your group is targeted as a hate group, but they got it wrong. And I believe that it's intentional."

"**NO SHIT**!" Yusuf couldn't contain the insult of the obvious that she was spewing to him.

"Please let me finish. I'm here to let you know that the FBI is watching you and your organization. They could also try to tie you to the gun ring in Chicago. They are trying to get whatever they can on you and your organization to shut you down. I just want you to be aware and please be careful."

"Thanks for the warning. Is that it?"

Yusuf had to maintain his defiance and sarcasm to let her know that she means nothing to him anymore. And that he doesn't trust her or anything she has to say. Toni understood, but she also needed to keep him on guard to protect him; the man she loved. Although, she was unable to relay that to him. But she wanted to do all that she could to protect him, in spite of his feelings towards her. She felt she gave him a fair enough warning to protect himself until she can find a way to protect him too.

# España

*Mateo.*

Toni arrives at BCN airport in Barcelona. She can't wait to enjoy the city and her Spanish lover again, and to get her mind off all the things going on in the states. Her feelings for a man who she wasn't supposed to fall for. The revelation that her parents were killed by her boss. The shock of finding out that she was left in the foster system to be abused. The fact that her uncle and aunt weren't really her uncle and aunt. It was enough to throw the average person over the edge, but Toni worked for an agency where deception, lies, assassination and death were all in a day's work.

Mateo sends a limousine for Toni. She arrives at the hotel and the porter takes her luggage from the car, then takes it to her room. It gets there before she gets to her room. She has to stop at the front desk to sign in and get her keycards and room number.

The suite is huge and has everything that she could need. She has a fully stocked bar with her favorite drinks, along with Mateo's favorites. There is a humidor stocked with wonderful cigars from around the world. She has a king-sized bed with the coziest looking bedspreads and pillows.

Toni walks into her gabinetto and it has marble floors and a marble shower, with marble sinks and bathtub. She notices there is a thermostat to adjust the floor heat and the base of the shower.

There's even an adjustable thermostat for the toilet seat. She also spots a jacuzzi in the back.

As Toni is unpacking, there is a knock on the door. She looks through the peephole. It is Mateo. Mateo is a tall, slim, gorgeous man, with dark curly hair, a mustache and chin beard. He has a short haircut with an olive complexion and dresses like a model in a fashion show. She opens the door.

"Hola, la meva amant sexy! Com has estat? T'ho he perdut aizí!"

(Translation: "Hello my sexy lover! How have you been? I've missed you so!")

Toni spoke to Mateo in Catalan. The common language in Barcelona.

"Sóc meravellós! Com has estat? Ets tan encantador com sempre."

("I'm wonderful, beautiful! How have you been? You're as lovely as ever!")

"També sóc meravellós! I gràcies, pel bonic complement i d'aquesta habitació excepcional!"

("I'm wonderful too! And thank you! For the sweet complement and this outstanding room!")

"Estàs molt ben rebut dama!"

("You are quite welcome beautiful lady!")

Toni will continue to speak in Catalan her entire trip to Barcelona. She prefers it. She loves the fact that it is an autonomous language and can't wait to go to Catalunya. The entire Catalunyan culture is unique and autonomous. Her occupation gives her an appreciation for the culture even more. It is why she made sure to learn the language. Those who don't know the language have less access to the culture.

"Mateo, can I have use of your villa in Catalunya?" ** (** All Catalan will be written in English from this point until the end of the chapter.)

"Of course, my love! It's waiting for you whenever you're ready to go."

"Thank you so much! I appreciate you!" Toni walks toward Mateo, grabs his face with both her hands, and gives him the sexiest kiss that she can give him, while sliding her hands to the back of his head to pull him deeply into the kiss. Mateo grabs her waist, picks her up, walks her over to the bed and lays her down on it.

He begins to disrobe, as Toni watches his every move to take in the look of his sleek and chiseled body and his darkly tanned skin. While she's enjoying Mateo's unwitting striptease, she is slowly removing her own clothes. She leaves on her sexy underwear to give Mateo the job of removing them.

"Turn around," says Mateo. "Let me see that ass through those sexy panties."

Toni has on black sheer underwear that is hugging her curves, perfectly and is giving him a nice peek-a-boo tantalization. Mateo grabs her from behind and pulls her to him while cupping and squeezing her breasts. He kisses her on the neck behind her right ear, then kisses the back of her neck right before he gently pushes her forward just enough to open the back of her bra.

As he is allowing her bra to drop to the floor, he positions his hands back to her front as he cups her breasts again and pinches her nipples. Toni winces, and lets out a sexy sigh that has Mateo's member poking her from the back. He then pulls her panties down to right beneath her bottom, then tells her to lay on the bed on her back. He slowly removes her panties.

Mateo likes to make love slowly and sensually and Toni appreciates the patience of intercourse with him. They are both nude when Mateo kisses Toni sensually as she kisses him back. He takes his time and kisses her ear and nibbles on it. Then he kisses her neck then licks and caresses it with his tongue. When he gets to her breasts he gently kisses and sucks each of them. He rubs and fondles one while he has the other's nipple in his mouth. He gives them both equal attention.

He then kisses down her belly then around her groin area and thighs. He licks her hips then flips her over to kiss her soft, round, sexy bottom. He loves her milk chocolate booty. He smacks it and watches it jiggle. It makes him hard as a rock. As he spreads her cheeks, Toni knows to toot her booty up in the air and grab her pillow.

Mateo took out a few personal wipes from the container by the bed. Toni could feel the cool wet wipes touch the top of the opening of her glutes, then slowly slide down to the base of her vagina. He used three wipes to thoroughly clean her anal area. She then felt his big hands spread her as much as he could, followed by his warm, wet licks as they started slowly from the top of her clitoris, to the opening of her vagina, several times.

She feels the softness of his oral muscle lick her from the base of her vaginal area, all the way to her anus, several times, before she feels the penetration of his long, fat, wet tongue enter her anus slowly and deeply. His tongue play finds spots in Toni that arouses her in a way that no one but Mateo has ever been able to find. He pleasures her for a couple of minutes as Toni holds on tightly to her pillow needing to find the relief of an orgasm.

Mateo finally gets back to her clitoris and covers it with his open mouth. He uses a light, tight suction as he takes his tongue with a steady back and forth lick until Toni's body jerks from the intense climax. Once her body stops jerking, he slides himself into her vagina then slowly pumps Toni. Her eyes are rolling up in her head from the slow pounding on her cervix and the spread of her vagina from the girth of his penis.

Toni orgasms several times before Mateo finds his release. Toni always knows when that is about to happen because Mateo has his own unique breathing before climaxing. He breathes really heavily right before and during an orgasm. Toni is always soaked afterwards.

Toni goes into the bathroom to clean herself up. Once she gets back to the bed Mateo is lying there with his eyes closed; she lays next to him. He then opens his eyes and lays on his side facing Toni.

"Your pussy is as delicious as ever, Love!"

"And your kisses, licks and fucks are as satisfying as ever, baby!"

"I have some things to do but I'm hoping that you'll have dinner with me tonight."

"I would love to Mateo!"

"Wonderful! I'll send my car for you around 8 O'clock."

"I'll wait for the call."

Mateo kisses Toni, jumps in the shower, then is on his way out the door.

"See you tonight, Love!"

"See you later, baby!"

*Casa Mila.*

The limo comes to pick up Toni and take her to Casa Milà, for great food then live jazz. Mateo meets Toni at the limousine, takes her arm and escorts her inside of Café de la Pedrera, for dinner. Then afterwards, she and Mateo would enjoy some live jazz on the rooftop of "La Padrera" (Casa Milà) in Barcelona.

"My you are breathtaking, Toni!"

"Thank you, Mateo! You're quite handsome yourself!"

Toni wanted to devour him right there. He was deliciously handsome and perfectly fit. She could hardly wait to enjoy him again, at the hotel tonight. But she knew that the lead up, from the food to the music, would make the sex even more climactic. She would enjoy every moment of it.

Once they are seated, Mateo already has a bottle of Toni's favorite Spanish sparkling wine on ice; Cava Gramona Cuvée Brut. She then orders the Tuna Tataki, which comes with celery and mini vegetables. Mateo orders the Veal Tenderloin Foie, which comes with mushrooms and fennel crudités. They end their meals with chocolate and vanilla mousse, with red berries and Oreo foam, respectively. Dinner was delectable!

After dinner, they make their way up to the roof to enjoy the live jazz concert. They thoroughly enjoy the music as they continue their drinks. They leave before the concert is over to avoid the crowds. They go down to the limo and Mateo rides back to the hotel with Toni. He escorts her up to her room but has to take care of some business. He tells her that he will be back in about an hour. "That's perfect," she thought, so that she could unwind, undress and set the tone for an easy mood and atmosphere.

When Mateo returns, Toni has on some nice soothing music by Paco De Lucia. And she is wearing one of the beautiful, sexy negligees that Mateo had in the closet for her.

"My, my, my… Beautiful! Just, beautiful!"

"Thank you, Mateo!"

He grabs Toni and they slow dance to the music, as he stares down at her. When the song ends, they sit down on the sofa. Toni brings the humidor over to the table, along with the bottle of sparkling wine and some cognac for Mateo; he likes Cardenal Mendoza Solera.

Toni pours his cognac as he lights up the cigars for them both. They begin to smoke and enjoy the cigars in a few minutes of silence, then they begin to talk.

"How have things been since I last saw you?" Says Mateo.

"All is well!" Toni doesn't like saying too much, although Mateo knows who and what she is. He also works in intelligence.

"That's good to hear. I presume you're between assignments?"

"You presume correctly!" Toni smiles, and Mateo understands to leave that conversation there.

"So, you're going to Catalunya? Should I join you at some point, or no?"

"Not this time, babe! I have some unfinished business that I need to take care of."

"Well, if you need me, just give a holler."

"I will."

Mateo moves closer to Toni and starts kissing her. Toni loves the cigar taste in his mouth; it turns her on. She brakes from the kiss and puts out her cigar. She is ready to get busy again. She removes her satin robe then kneels between Mateo's legs. She arches her face up as a signal for him to kiss her. He holds his cigar to the side, grabs the back of her head with his left hand and kisses her deeply. This takes her to where she needs to go.

Mateo sits back with cigar in hand and takes a deep puff. Toni unbuckles his belt and unzips his pants while making steady eye contact with him. She tugs at his pants so that he will rise up enough for her to pull them down, then removes them, along with his underwear.

She uses her hand to cup his penis and roll it against her cheek. She then rolls it from her right cheek, across her lips, then to her left cheek and back. She rolls it back to her lips then begins to give it strong passion sucks from the base of his penis, to his frenulum. She then uses her tongue to lick his frenulum, then put the head of his penis into her mouth. She uses her tongue to continue her massage of his prepuce.

Mateo lays back with his eyes closed enjoying her attentiveness. He takes puffs of his cigar here and there until he needs to concentrate on the pleasure of Toni's expertise; he puts out his cigar. Mateo is extremely large, and Toni does her best to get as much of him into her mouth as she can. But she knows the best method of taking him all the way in. The best position to perform deep throat.

She grabs Mateo by the hand, leads him to the bed and tells him to stand at the side of the bed. While he's waiting for her to get into position, he takes off the rest of his clothes. Toni just loves his fit muscular physique and she is hot and wet just looking at him nude, and thinking 'That dick of his, **LAWD**, is a beauty!'

Toni removes her gown and is nude as she lays on her back and allows her head to hang over the side of the bed in the perfect position to take in Mateo's length and girth. She reaches up to grab and guide his member into her mouth and throat. As she pulls it into her mouth, she relaxes her gag reflex once it hits the tip of her throat. She then continues to guide it as Mateo bends over and helps to push it as far in as he can.

He lets it sit there for a moment as he pulls her legs up and open and he puts his mouth over her clit and begins to tongue it. He then begins to invade her throat slow and steady. He knows that she can hold her breath for a couple of minutes, so he gets several good thrusts in before he pulls out to let her get her breath.

When her breathing slows down, she grabs his bottom to let him know to go again. He does. He continues to pleasure her clit, while he slowly prods her throat again. He has to stop pleasuring her because he is ready to come. He picks up the pace of his throat thrusts, with steady and even pumps until he explodes down her esophagus and empties himself inside of her. He pulls back just enough for her to catch her breath and get a taste of his semen.

As his penis sits on her tongue, he continues his cunnilingus until Toni orgasms clitorally. Once they are both finished their oral pleasuring, they lay at the head of the bed and fall asleep.

*Mercedes.*

Before Toni leaves Barcelona, she needs to go see a young lady she befriended the last time she was there; she went to visit Mercedes. As she was waiting for the door to be answered, Toni thought back on the day that she had beat Mercedes husband up severely. He treated Mercedes badly, and he would beat on her, often.

Toni met her one day at Park Güell. She was just sitting on some steps looking sad as Toni was about to walk up the steps. Toni also noticed her black eye and the bruises on her arms.

"Are you okay?" Said Toni. "You look so sad…"

"I'm okay." Said Mercedes as she looked up at the beautiful brown lady with the pretty, curly hair. Toni didn't want to offend her or make her feel embarrassed about her black eye and bruises, so she asked her where she could find the mosaic frog. Mercedes gave her directions, but Toni played like she was confused and couldn't follow them.

"Could you walk with me, please? I'm an American tourist and I would appreciate it if you helped me to find it. I'll gladly pay you."

"You don't have to pay me. I'll show you."

"My name is Toni. What is your name, if you don't mind me asking?"

"Not at all. I'm Mercedes."

"Pleased to meet you Mercedes."

Toni extended her hand and Mercedes shook it. Mercedes walked Toni to where the mosaic frog was. Toni asked her to take a picture of her next to the frog, so she did.

"Can I please treat you to lunch, since you won't let me pay you? Actually, I would love the company. Please?" Toni was hoping to get Mercedes to want to open up. Mercedes agreed to have lunch with the lonely American. They sat and ate, and Toni made up a story about an ex-boyfriend. And how he used to hit on her and how she got away from him. She was still hoping to get Mercedes to open up.

Toni had a soft spot for abused women. She remembered how she felt as a little girl, lonely in the foster care system, being molested and abused over and over. Flashes of the fear she felt, the pain she went through, and the shame she carried around for years passed through her mind. She was determined to find out what caused Mercedes bruises. Especially since she was a kind and sweet woman. Something she was able to determine in the little bit of time spent with her. She wouldn't find out the truth that day, but she had a plan in mind.

Toni talked Mercedes into taking a selfie with her, just for her own memories. Not for social media or anything like that. She told her that she wanted to remember her. Toni had a lot of connections in Barcelona. She used the picture to show it to a few locals who she knew. She wanted to find out how Mercedes got her black eye and bruises. One of her connects knew exactly who she was, and how she got her bruises. It was her "piece of shit, abusive husband." Toni was livid.

She made it her business to find out everything that she could about Juan. She found out where they lived, where he worked, where he hung out, who his friends were and who his family was. She had no interest in finding out why he became abusive scum; only how to keep him from abusing Mercedes. Trying to get her to leave him would take more time and patience than Toni had to give.

Toni got word where he was hanging out one night. She also got word that he had beaten on Mercedes that same night. First, she called up Mercedes to check on her, to make sure that she was okay. She sounded a bit sad but said that she was fine. She didn't want to frighten her by showing up at her door, so she had flowers sent while she sat across the street from her home to try and get a glimpse of her. She wanted physical proof that she was okay.

As the flowers were being delivered by an associate of Toni's, she had her binoculars up as he knocked on Mercedes door. She was watching so that she could get a good look at Mercedes. She knew that she was the only one home, based on her informant's report.

There was a pretty long wait before she answered the door and Toni became concerned. She had the flower deliverer call Mercedes on the phone to let her know that he was outside. The flowers were given anonymously, so she wasn't worried about her being too nervous about the phone call wondering how they got her number. It obviously had to be someone she knew.

When Mercedes finally opened the door, she mostly stood behind the door. Toni got a better view for a couple of seconds once Mercedes had to grab the flowers. She seemed to be limping and had bruises on her arm. That's all the fire Toni needed to beat a warning into her husband.

Toni didn't have the patience to wait for him to leave the bar he was at, so she decided to catch him on his way to work in the morning. She knew his car and waited for him while leaning on a pole near his car. As he approached, he had on a baseball cap and had his head down in his phone. She needed confirmation that he was Juan.

"Juan Toledano?" Said Toni.

Juan lifted his head and gave Toni the proof that she needed that it was him.

"Who wants to know?" Juan said with all the arrogance Toni needed to beat him to a pulp; and that she did.

He didn't have enough time to even gauge what was going on in order to get a good chance to fight back. Toni beat him into two black eyes and two broken ribs.

"You, insignificant piece of shit you!!! If you ever touch Mercedes again, you will lose your life as you know it; and that is a literal promise. And don't you ever mention this conversation to her, or I will know about it and I will fuck you up again, but worse. And I will continue to do it until there is no more you."

Toni quickly left before he could get his bearings or really understand what just happened. Once he did, he had no idea who could have done such a thing to him, but he took her words to heart.

Toni remembered how she wanted him to feel what he was doing to his wife. He promised that he'd never do it again. But Toni found out that he was still beating Mercedes and it had become even worse.

Toni knocks on the door. Mercedes opens the door and is happy to see Toni and gives her a big hug. She invites her in, and they sit down in the living room on the sofa, side by side.

"How are you, Beautiful?" Toni made sure that her every word to a battered woman was positive, empowering and complimentary.

"I'm okay Toni! How are you? How have you been?"

"I'm fantastic! About to go to Catalunya for a few days and enjoy some of the Correfoc festivals. You want to come with me?"

"I wish that I could, but I'm too busy with work."

"Too bad Honey. If you can find some time, just give me a call, okay? Here… let me get your phone number and I will text you mine."

Mercedes tells Toni her number, then sends her number to Mercedes.

"Okay, got it!"

They sat and talked about different little things going on in each other's lives and reminisced about the fun they had in the past. Neither one of them mentioned Juan, Mercedes' husband. Toni wasn't concerned about him recognizing her either. Her look was always different, and she was confident that he wouldn't know that she was the same person that beat him up years before.

Toni could see pain in Mercedes eyes but remained upbeat. She also didn't want to do or say anything or encourage Mercedes to do or say anything that could get her in a verbal or physical confrontation with Juan when she left. They had a nice visit, hugged and kissed, then Toni left.

Toni knew that Juan was in the house. She could feel Mercedes' fear. Toni would catch him outside of the house sooner or later, and this time he wasn't going to make it back home in the same condition. He had his warning and his chance. She had also seen pictures that came from the hospital. Mercedes was lucky to be alive.

# Catalunya

*Les festes.*

Toni went to Catalunya right in the middle of a Correfoc festival. Catalunyans would go all out with celebrations since the end of Franco's reign. Franco forbid not only the Correfoc festivals, but everything about the Catalunyan culture; including the language. He banned it all and made it illegal. Spanish was the only language they could legally speak. But the Catalunyans never stopped speaking their language. They just kept it behind closed doors and underground. Now, they celebrate their culture with great pride.

Toni loved the energy and darkness of the Correfocs, which dates back to the 1100's and the "Ball de Diables" (The Devils' Dance). She loved everything about Catalunya and its rich culture. Especially the fact that they weren't very fond of outsiders. She had eased her way in years before by learning the culture and the language. She made many friends and connections over the years. She felt a homelike ease and relaxation when she wasn't there on business.

So, Toni went to the villa and she only brought a minimum amount of clothing. She would enjoy the festival, but she had a specific goal for her stay this time. Before she left the states, Toni got word of a pedophile priest who was hiding out in Catalunya.

He was a maintenance worker at a church there. This is the priest who molested one of her closest childhood friends.

Johnny was an altar boy when he was a child. This priest would molest him often for about a year. As Johnny grew older, he began having sexual tendencies toward young boys. Tendencies that he fought against. Tendencies that he never gave into. Tendencies that would cause him to take his life. He left a note that identified the priest, Johnny's constant battle within himself, and his ultimate decision to relieve him from his demons.

Johnny's death and note wouldn't be the catalyst to end this priests' career in the U.S. But there would be an eventual case against him in the years after Johnny's death, by many men who were raped by this priest as children. He was removed from his position and sentenced to do time. He illegally left the country before he would set foot inside a prison cell.

Word was that the priest was given a job at this church in Catalunya and he started befriending young alter-boys from the church he was allowed to work at. As far as Toni's contacts knew, he hadn't molested any of them yet, but his behaviors were consistent with the actions of a pedophile grooming a boy for sex. She had a gift for him.

In the meantime, Toni had people watching for Juan and to let her know when he was in a place where she could get to him. Juan had gotten inebriated and came out to enjoy the festival; Toni got word. She was told exactly where he was. She had many connections in Catalunya, so she made a phone call and had a devil's "uniform" delivered to her on a street corner, also the fireworks she would need to blend in. She wouldn't allow anyone to come to Mateo's villa.

The "uniform" was the perfect cover during a Correfoc. Toni got dressed and went to the festival through a back way so that no one would see her approaching the crowd. She had her wireless earphones on as she talked to the person following Juan.

"He has on a red baseball cap, a black t-shirt with red writing, jeans and black tennis shoes." Said the voice in the phone.

Toni is walking around with her fireworks and her hood on her head, to prevent the sparks from burning her hair. She blends right in with the rest of the devils. She waits for a bit more direction to identify where Juan is in the crowd.

"He's close to the devils on the side of the street near the park."

Toni spots him. She takes her time getting over to him. He's walking around but mostly within a 10-foot range. She walks up to him face to face.

"Remember me?"

Juan stood in place with a confused look on his face. Toni pulled out and revealed a six-inch switchblade. She grabbed Juan as if to hug him but put him in a front bear hug hold in which he couldn't escape; he wasn't a big man. She then punched the blade into his lower back and severed his spine; as she pulled the blade from one side of his lower backbone to the other, with the precision of a surgeon. It happened so fast that Juan was in a daze.

She grabbed both his upper arms from the front, then whispers in his ear,

"If you ever put your hands on your wife again, I will make sure that your paralysis spreads from your neck down."

She then pushes him back and down onto the bench that was a couple of feet behind him. Juan is in shock unable to speak a word, eventually losing consciousness from the pain and the loss of blood.


"Call for an ambulance before he bleeds out."

Toni speaks into her wireless headset aware that her contact is watching her every move. She wants to make sure that he doesn't die but made sure that his paralysis would stop him from harming his wife. In the least, she knew that it would slow him down so that Mercedes could learn to get the upper hand on any situation of potential violence from him again.

She pulled his hat down over his face so that he looked like someone who fell asleep on the bench.

As she walked away, she didn't hear anything to suggest that anyone knew what had just happened. She removed the devil's uniform once she got away from the crowd and in the spot where she was directed to go. She threw the uniform in a trash can, grabbed the small bottle of lighter fluid left behind the trash can by her connect, then lit it on fire. No big deal during the fiery festival.

Toni would not go back to see Mercedes because she already knew that she would be distraught. She loved her husband in spite of his abuse. But he had been warned and Toni fulfilled her promise to him.

The next morning, when Toni knew that the priest was at work, she got into his home and checked for his EpiPen's. He was highly allergic to shellfish, so he always had two. Toni had brought two pre-filled pens with her. She only found one of his, so she switched it out with one of her special pens. She needed to get her hands on the other pen before she could fulfill her plan. He must've had it on him. Most people didn't keep their EpiPen's on their person, so she needed to find out where he kept his personals at work. She found out that the maintenance workers had lockers.

She decided to enjoy the festivals the rest of that day and would follow him to work in the morning. She got up early that morning and watched him from her car across the street from where he lived. He walked to work so she quietly got out of her car and followed him. He was clueless. Once he went into the church, Toni followed behind him and saw where his locker was. She hung out in the bathroom until she was certain that he had begun his workday.

Her training provided her with skills to have no problem opening his locker. She rummaged through his things and found his other EpiPen and switched it out. She could now finish her plan. She went back to his home then put an odorless highly concentrated liquid of shellfish in his coffee grounds. Thanks to the same scientists who made the special EpiPen's with the same shellfish concentration that went into his coffee. So, when he attempted to use the EpiPen, he would get another dose of the same highly toxic allergen. Who cared how long it would take for someone to find his body? Nothing was traceable.

# Back on U.S. Soil

*Tom.*

Toni's first concern when she got back on U.S. soil, was how much information Liz found on Tom. She found all kinds of random information, so Toni collected it all to see if any of it connected; or if she could use it to possibly protect her life if the need arose in the future. And given all of the recent revelations that she uncovered; the future was near.

One of the things that fueled a specific curiosity, was that her mother's rape was about 8 1/2 months before she was born. She thought maybe she could've been born early. So, Toni wondered if it were possible that Tom could be her biological father. She didn't know if this was a good thing or bad thing at this point, but she needed to know for sure, one way or another.

Toni called Tom for an appointment to find out when her next assignment would be. When she got to his office, she needed to find some easy DNA in order to have it tested to see if he could possibly be her father. He wasn't in his office yet, so she had to wait until he got there; his administrative assistant let her in. Toni didn't sit down right away. She was looking around the office to see if there was anything that she could use for a DNA test.

She checked his chair and desk for possible hair strands. She then went into his personal bathroom to look for some hair strands, too. She found a comb in the drawer with what looked like his gray hair. She took it off the comb and put it in a small zip lock bag. She brought it with her just for this reason. Tom came in while she was in the rest room. She flushed the toilet and washed her hands so that she didn't seem suspicious.

"Well, hello there Antonaya! How was your vacation?"

"Toni, sir! It was wonderful!"

"Barcelona? I bet it was!"

"Yes, it's a beautiful city! Are there any new assignments yet?" Toni wasn't in the mood for chit chat.

"Well, before we get to that, why don't you tell me about Juan Toledano and Javier Gallegos, the former priest? I would hate to think that you've become a rogue agent. Are you a rogue agent Ms. Rice?"

('Ms. Rice? Hmmm…' Toni thought. She didn't know what to make out of this twist of her name from him.)

Toni thought that she took care of those issues under the radar.

"Well, Sir…" Toni explained her reasons for crippling Juan and taking out Javier. Tom wasn't happy about it, but he only reprimanded her and told her to never make those kinds of decisions again without his knowledge of them.

"By the way," said Tom, "no one has a clue about what really happened to Gallegos. And Juan's attack was reported as a random act of violence. He claims that he didn't see the perpetrators face.

Gallegos death was considered as a severe allergic reaction, so they didn't investigate the incident any further."

Charlie just smirked. "And the assignment sir?"

"Nothing yet, but soon."

"Any hints of where it will be? In the states? Europe? The islands? Africa?"

"Nothing for sure, but it looks like it will be in the states."

Toni let out a sigh. "Really? It's been a while since I had an assignment out of the country."

"Yeah, well, we need you where we need you." Toni twisted her mouth to that answer.

"Okay then, well, let me know."

"Will do, Antonaya!"

"Toni, sir."

"Right! Talk to you soon. Have a great day."

Toni left with disappointment on her face and in her voice, but she got what she really came for. She needed to have a rushed DNA test, so she went to a lab she used for some of her assignments. She didn't let them know whose hair she was using, other than checking to see if the person is her father. She got it back the next day.

Toni went to Shomely to tell him the results and discuss her next move. Then she went to Liz to tell her about the test results. She had a lot to think about. Were the results going to help her or hurt her? She wasn't sure at this point, so she needed to think deeply about it and take her time figuring it all out.

Toni needed to know whether Tom had any children, whether he liked children, if he ever wanted children; just how he felt about offspring in general. She would put Liz to task again to find out. Liz came back with: he didn't have any children, he didn't want any children because of his occupation, but he loved children. Toni deduced that was probably why she was still alive, but that didn't explain why he left her for harm.

Another bit of information came to light, too. Come to find out, it wasn't Tom who left her in the system. It was the same guy who had information on Tom; Joe Saban. So, now Toni is wondering if Tom really had her parents killed. She needed to dig deeper to figure out what was really the truth.

So, Toni goes back to Shomely and Liz and tells them what she thinks; she needs Shomely's advice and Liz's help again. They also want to know the truth. Liz has no problem continuing to dig for answers. She warned Toni that it might take a few months. She had no choice but to wait, although she needed to find a way to protect Yusuf very soon; time was running out.

Toni decided to go with her instincts and took a chance at confronting Tom. She needed leverage in order to protect herself. And Yusuf's protection was contingent upon her own safety. She made an appointment with him and told him that the reason for the meeting was personal. He didn't think twice about what that could have meant.

The next day, Toni is in his office and begins the conversation.

"Tom, did you know my mother?"

"Who was your mother, Antonaya?"

"Toni, sir! Her name was Charlene Trautman."

"Charlene Trautman?" It didn't ring a bell with Tom.

"Her maiden name was Pierce."

"Charlene Pierce, Charlene Peirce." Tom stopped saying the name then looked Toni right in her eyes. He was silent for several seconds.

"Charlene was your mother?" He seemed to be shocked by the news.

"Yes!"

"Wait! I have your file, Toni! I know your story and Charlene is not a part of it."

"Well, she was my mother."

Tom just stared at Toni without saying a word. He couldn't rap his head around the information that she just told him.

"Toni, I need to do some research. This isn't good. I should know everything about you."

"Sir, that's not all!"

Tom just stared at Toni not knowing what was going to come next. He just sat and waited for her to say what was on her mind.

"I'm your daughter."

Tom stared at her, expressionless.

"I know this is hard for you to believe, but I had a DNA test done. I took some hair from your comb in your bathroom the last day that I was here. The test came back positive."

Tom started remembering his last time with Charlene. He remembered the date and everything, because it was their last time together. He remembered that she came to his law office front to say a final goodbye to him. He wanted them to be together in spite of her marriage, but she told him no, because she really loved her husband. They ended up having an intimate moment to say goodbye which ended up in a sexual interlude. She told him that it could not ever happen again, then left. He was heart-broken but understood and accepted it. He just wanted her to be happy.

These were his thoughts and memories. He didn't tell any of this to Toni. He remained quiet.

"What do you have to say about this?" Said Toni.

"I don't know what to say right now, except that we need to go together to get this DNA test. Then we can go from there."

They went together to a different lab right away. They had to wait a few hours to get the results back, so Tom went back to his office and told Toni that he would call her when he got back the results. Toni wasn't sure what to think about the information that led her to believe what she did about Tom, initially. She didn't get the feeling that he knew anything. Even though they were trained to dupe people, she really didn't feel that's what was going on here.

Tom called Toni, "The test is back!"

"What is the result?"

"Meet me at the coffee shop." Toni knew which one. It was code for a specific coffee shop.

"Can't you tell me now, sir?" Toni is anxious, but isn't sure why, since she already had the test done.

"No, meet me at the shop."

Toni shows up to the coffee shop.

"Take a seat Anton… Toni."

"Thank you, sir."

"So, first off, the test came back positive that you're my daughter. Secondly, I did some research and found out that what you told me is true. I also found out some interesting information that I was unaware of. Somehow, Joe Saban is involved in all this. I still have to find out how and why."

Neither one of them know how to handle the information that she is his daughter, so they stick to business. Toni doesn't want to let him know any more of what she's uncovered. She doesn't want to put Shomely and Liz in harms' way. His eventual revelations will actually give her an even better understanding for whose side

Tom is really on, so she will wait to hear what he finds out and compare it to what she already knows.

Tom's spy senses became sharpened with all the new information that he had acquired. He hadn't done field work in many years, but all of this would force him out of his office and back into agent mode.

*Agent Tom.*

Tom needs to do some investigating of Joe Saban, but he doesn't want to alert him to anything. He also went to Liz to see if she could hack into Joe's files. His direction was for her to find every and anything about Charlene Pierce, Charlene Trautman, Antonaya Price and anything about himself. Liz understood and assured him that she would find everything that she could. She also realized that she would probably have to get into files above Joe Saban to find out who *he* truly is.

Tom did some digging around himself and he called in several street favors. He needed to know who Joe Saban was outside of the agency. He found out that he isn't well liked, he is a notorious racist, he has ties to a hate group, and he is an undercover sexual sadist. The streets know all of his personal dirt.

He frequents an underground bordello, where any type of fetish or perversion can be met. He uses an alias, but they know who he is because he had threatened to bust them if they ever prevented him from using their establishment. The owner checked him out and found out who he really is.

They never tried to keep him away because they didn't need the heat; even though they knew he was a racist sadist prick. He would always ask for Black girls and they always had to give him the new girls, because no one who had experienced him ever wanted a second experience. A couple of the girls quit when they were about to be forced to deal with him again. And these were girls who dealt with sadists all the time.

Tom wanted to know what he could possibly be doing to these women for them to have such a reaction to him. The owner eventually talked a couple of girls into telling Tom. It was really hard because most of them were too afraid to. So, Tom interviewed the two girls separately. The first girl, Lickerish, had very dark, beautiful, smooth skin. She was model tall and slim with long silky hair to her waist.

She said, "He played Russian roulette with me. He put a bullet in the chamber of a really big gun. He then stuck it in my mouth and made me suck on it. If I stopped, he pushed it as deep into my mouth as he could, then pulled the trigger. I just knew that I was going to die that day.

Then he handcuffed me to the bed and fucked me with the barrel of the same gun with the bullet still in it. I was terrified that it was going to go off, because he fucked me with it so hard and so long that I was bloody afterwards. Then he urinated on me to clean the blood off.

After that, he told me to open my mouth then he sat his stinking ass on my face and tried to shit in my mouth. I closed it and I almost suffocated from the amount of shit that he smashed all over my face because he was rocking back and forth on it." She was in tears telling her story.

"When he was done, he kept smacking me in the face for not eating his shit. He hit me so hard and so many times that my face was bloody, sore and bruised. He then jerked off and came all over my shitty face." She had to stop for a few seconds as she silently cried. "After he removed the handcuffs, he forced me to clean him off and clean the bed up before I could wash my face." She was in tears and couldn't say anymore, so Tom didn't force her.

Once he interviewed the next girl, she told a very similar story and that was enough for Tom. He thanked the girls for their bravery and assured them that nothing would happen to them for telling their stories. He also thanked the owner and let him know that this was between them.

When Liz came back with the file about Tom raping Charlene and then having her and her husband killed, he was mortified. He loved Charlene and had a really hard time after her death, even though he went to work every day. He wasn't supposed to let anything get to him in the way that her death did, so he faked his way through until he got to a place of peace.

He wondered why the file existed, and why was it still around so many years after the supposed incident? And why would Joe try to harm him? He needed answers but had to find the right recourse to get them. He would go through all the files that Liz found for him and also everything that he could access. He contacted as many people as he could discreetly and couldn't find out why Joe targeted him. So, he decided to confront Joe. And he had an endgame if things went bad.

*Joe Saban.*

Tom had the owner of the underground Bordello to call him when Joe came back. Tom needed to confront Joe in a place where he could back him up against a wall. He assured the owner that he didn't have anything to worry about. He promised, no negative repercussions. So, when Joe came in, the owner called Tom right away. Tom told him to delay any girls from going into his room and that he'd be there in 20 minutes. The owner said he'd do his best.

When Tom got there, he received a nod and a piece of paper from the owner. The paper said the red room. He didn't need a key because the doors remained unlocked until the girls entered. Tom entered the room and Joe had an arrogant smirk on his face.

"What the hell are you doing here, Tom?"

"I need to talk to you."

"About what?" Joe walked over to the dresser, away from Tom, and sat on it.

"About why you have a file on me saying that I killed Charlene Trautman."

Joe gave a little laugh.

"Because you fell in love with that Black bitch. What the fuck was wrong with you? How can you fall in love with any of those animals?"

"Animals? Aren't you waiting for one of those so-called animals to fuck at this very moment?"

Joe laughed again. "If you knew what I do to these monkey bitches, you wouldn't even have said that out of your mouth. I don't fuck 'em. Not like you did."

"What did who I was in love with have to do with you? Why did you kill her and her husband? Why did you lie in that file?" Tom just needed confirmation that Joe killed Charlene and her husband, although he knew that it was him.

"She was married to another monkey lover. And he was always trying to pass laws for those people. I promised some people that I owed a favor to, that I'd take care of it. He was the target. She was just for the pleasure of killing a blackie."

Tom's reserve was commendable, but he was enraged on the inside. He needed to know the entire truth.

"Why leave the little girl in foster homes to be molested and abused? We're supposed to protect the kids. Where's your humanity, man?"

"Humanity? Are you fucking kidding me? We've killed and have people killed for a living." Joe lunges his torso forward as he stares Tom in the face (still at a far enough distance), at the audacity of his comment.

"Where's *your* fucking humanity? Oh! Wait! You have none." Joe rolls his eyes and sits back.

"Besides, we do all of this research and know what makes a perfect agent. I created the perfect agent in Antonaya, wouldn't you say?" Joe smiles sarcastically.

"There has to be a limit to who we harm and kill, or else we're no better than the worst murderers out there."

"And do you really think that we *are* better? There's a reason why I'm the best at what I do. I keep the upper hand by being willing to go further than the rest of you pansies."

"*One* of the best. And wanting to protect innocent children doesn't make anyone a pansy. It makes them a worthwhile human being." Tom wanted to let him know that he's one of the best, too; even without the over the top inhumanities.

Both men knew that they both weren't going to walk back out that door. And both men planned on themselves being the one to walk out. Each of them had several weapons on them. They stared at each other in silence for about a minute. Then there were two gunshots.

# A New Assignment

## A Visit Home.

Toni decided that it was time to visit her parents. The parents who raised her. The parents who created the woman she is today. She still had a key to her parent's home. She knew they were both home because their cars were there. It was the perfect time for her to get the answers she needed.

As she drove into the neighborhood that she was raised in, a flood of memories came into her head. Mostly the high school years and the friends she made, along with the non-friends who attempted to give her a hard time. She could never get really close to anyone, but those she called friend were always there for her and pulled her out to parties and activities that she always ended up enjoying. A few of them were even in some of the self-defense and weapons classes she attended. None were Black though.

As she opened the door with her key, the smell in the vestibule brought back even more memories. This was home for Toni. Her safe haven. The place where she felt loved and protected. The place that brought her eventual peace of mind. The place where she might have to break permanent ties if she didn't get the answers she was seeking and hoping for.

Her mother was in the kitchen, cooking.

"Hi mom! Where's dad?"

Her mother was surprised and happy to see her. They walked towards each other, hugged and kissed.

"He's in his office."

"Okay, I need to talk to you guys. It's important."

"Alright! Let me go get him. Have a seat on the sofa, Toni."

Her mother went to get her father. Toni stood up when he entered the room, then hugged and kissed him. They all sat down.

"What's this about Toni?" Said her father.

"I know the real story of how I came to be with you guys. And that I was *targeted* for spy-hood." Toni had no patience for 'beating around the bush.'

"Please don't deny anything because I've already talked to Tom about it.

So… What's your side of the story? Please be honest with me. As a matter of fact, I have some specific questions. How could you mold an innocent child to become a spy?"

"Toni…" Her father attempted to interject, but Toni kept talking.

"I know that you two worked for the intelligence agency too, but how could you do that to a child?"

"Let me answer this." Said her father.

"Toni, we did work for the intelligence agency, so you know that we had a job to do and we did it. It doesn't mean that we didn't come to love you as our own child. We also felt that we helped you to become strong enough to take on this world. It's a really cruel world out there. And we knew about the abuse that you suffered, we put you in therapy to help you cope with that."

"Really!" Said Toni. "You mean that the agency had me put into therapy after leaving me to be raped and abused in the foster system. All of this was in my files, so I know the truth."

"Yes… The agency had us put you into therapy. We had nothing to do with you being left in foster care. We were assigned to you when they decided to get you out of there."

Toni's mother chimed in. "Toni, your father and I were chosen to raise you, because we wanted children but couldn't have any. We truly love each other, and we are really married. We weren't spies. We just worked for intelligence. We served the agency as a psychiatrist and psychologist.

Honey, we couldn't love you anymore if you were our own child. When we first got you, yes, it was our job, but you were the saddest little thing and we wanted to bring some joy and happiness to your life. Our job was to help you heal and also to help you to become one of the best intelligence agents we could. Even though we had a job to do, we felt like we were preparing you to handle the world and anything that it threw at you."

"You do know that spies have a high mortality rate, don't you?" Said Toni.

"Well, it depends on the types of assignments that you get. We've always tried to influence your assignments and to try to make sure that you got the least dangerous ones."

"That's probably why they keep me in the states, so much. But, how am I supposed to feel about all this? I really don't know. We are in a world where you lie for a living. How do I know that you two are telling me the truth? And how am I to really feel about the way that I was raised and the reason for all this? I just don't know.

I'm also letting you know that I am going to need some time to figure all this out. Here's your keys for now. And please, let me call you when I'm ready. And I'd appreciate it, if don't call me before then."

Her parents seemed deeply saddened by it all, but Toni still wasn't sure if it were just an act. She still needed answers and needed time for everything to sink in. A lot of stunning information has been revealed in a short amount of time. She needed to process it all and knew that there was more to come that she would have to handle.


### Toms Daughter.

"Get out of the agency? Why would I do that? It's what I know. It's who I am and I'm good at it. I can't change the things that I've done or the things that I've seen. What would I do? Find a man and get married, buy a house with a white picket fence and have two and a half kids and a dog? The so-called American dream? Yeah, right! That's not *my* dream. I would wither away and die in that lifestyle. Death by excitement and living on the edge of life suits me much better. Thanks! But no thanks! I'll stick to my day job."

Toni is almost insulted by the suggestion of leaving the life that she knows and is good at. She even enjoys it. Tom suggested that maybe she would want to leave the agency given the revelations of how she was created and influenced to become a spy. Toni can't see herself doing anything else. Nor can she imagine a life as exciting as hers.

Being someone's wife, and or someone's mother doesn't suit her fancy at all. The thought of it is depressing to her. She doesn't think that it would have been for her even if she hadn't been created for the job. In some twisted way, she's almost grateful for the opportunity, although she would give it all up to have her parents back. Since that can never happen, being a spy is who she is for now, until.

"So, what happened to Joe Saban?" Asked Toni.

"He just disappeared. No one knows where he is." Said Tom. "But you'll never have to worry about him again." Toni knew better than to ask any more questions. She was good with that answer.

Toni took this opportunity to attempt to find a way to protect Yusuf. This was always at the back of her mind and she stayed conscious of every possible occasion that occurred, where she might influence this to happen.

"Tom?"

Tom was rifling through papers on his desk, then looking and typing into his computer, when Toni decided to ask him some questions.

"Yes?" Said Tom as he continued what he was doing and never looked toward Toni.

"May I ask what's going on with Yusuf Halim and the Chicago assignment?"

Tom freezes as he stares at Toni.

"No, you may not! You know that's not how things work." Tom looks at her to try to understand her motive for asking the question.

"Why are you inquiring Toni? This is highly unusual. What's going on here?"

She explained to him that Yusuf's organization was not what they labeled it to be. And that he wasn't who they claimed he was.

He stopped her from going any further.

"What's this about, Toni? Yusuf is an FBI target now. Our job was complete once the Chicago crew was arrested. He is no longer a concern of ours."

"Yes, sir." She was hoping that she didn't cause herself any trust issues with him. She decided to back down for now, but she was concerned about Yusuf's future and the future of his organization. She had to let it go for now.

Tom had the feeling that Toni may have developed some feelings for Yusuf. That wasn't good. He would also check into her claims, because even though she was out of line, he did respect her judgement based on all her past assignments. And with all that he found out about Joe Saban; he wasn't too sure of anything that he had his hand in. He may have even influenced the FBI to put Yusuf on the watch list as a threat to the U.S., in addition to using him as an unwitting asset. And Joe was also the one who recruited Toni.

So, Tom did his research and used his influence with some top FBI officials to reconsider Yusuf as a threat and informed them that Joe was no longer with the agency. He presented a good case to the right officials. It took a couple of months, but they reviewed all documentations and surveillance and agreed that he wasn't the threat they originally thought him to be. And they had already conceded that he was unaware of the gun ring in Chicago.

Tom would call Toni into his office and tell her that Yusuf was off the watch list. He was free to do his community work without the threat of being watched or charged with being any kind of hate organization. Toni was elated and needed to get the news to Yusuf. She didn't have to use a burner phone or use secret names or go to secret places. She was almost disappointed, but wasn't really, because the man she cared about was now safe. At least from the intelligence agencies.

She went to his community office to see him and tell him the news. Yusuf wasn't sure why she was there. The last time he saw her, she claimed the meeting with him put her life in danger. What's the story this time? He thought.

"Hello!" Said Toni.

"Hello." Yusuf responded practically emotionless.

"I'm here to pass on some good news. You're no longer on the watch list. They know that you're no threat and that you are just helping your community."

"Really? How'd that happen?"

Yusuf accepted the good news with skepticism and relief. Skepticism of how it may have happened, but with relief that it did.

"I guess they just realized that they were wasting their time based on whatever feedback they were getting."

"So, I guess that includes your feedback? Do I need to thank you for that?"

He had a lot of reluctance in wanting to give Toni any credit, but he knew that he was being watched even before she came on the scene. His anger also seems to have mellowed over time.

"Not at all! I'm just passing on the good news. Hopefully, this gives you at least some kind of relief."

"Yeah... Hopefully it will."

"Great! I hope that you have a wonderful day, Yusuf."

"Thank you! And likewise."

Toni left, just grateful that she was able to deliver the good news without an altercation this time. And she was happy to give Yusuf a reprieve from the many months of the threat of jail and death. As she walked away, she realized that she had many good memories from the assignment, and she learned so much about her culture and its history. She had Yusuf to thank for every bit of that. She'd be sure to send him a postcard one day from one of her overseas assignment destinations, to let him know just how much their time together meant to her. For now, she was just thankful for the peaceful moment she had with Yusuf.

### Joe's Replacement.

Tom called Toni in for a meeting. He was introducing Toni to Joe Saban's replacement.

"Toni, this is Felix Resnit! The new operations officer. Felix, this is Antonaya Rice. Call her Toni."

"A pleasure to meet you, sir!"

"Likewise, Ms. Rice."

They begin to discuss all of the changes that will be happening. Toni continues to listen to the plans that are going to be implemented, without a clear idea of what her next assignment would be. She is then released from the meeting as Tom and Felix continue to talk. Toni drops a pin dot bug in Tom's trash can.

She only needed to know what else was being discussed. She needed to find a way to get an overseas assignment, soon. She was a CIA agent, not FBI. She didn't want to continue FBI types of assignments anymore. No more international crimes on American soil for her. Let some newbie take those assignments. She needed more as she recalled the few overseas assignments that she was involved in.

Tom and Felix discussed an extremely dangerous detail over in Italy. The discussion was about deciding on which female agent to send, because this assignment would call for a highly skilled operative. He put the *who* in the hands of Tom since he knew the agents well. Tom needed to think on it.

Toni felt as though this was her in. Even though this would be an extremely dangerous mission, she knew the apparent risks and that she would have to remain on high alert her entire time through the assignment. Now her dilemma was how to get the assignment without them knowing that she was listening in.

Toni went to Tom's office the next day to ask about her next assignment. She was once again assigned to an international crime that was taking place on American soil.

"Why am I still getting assignments in the states. Can't I trade assignments with someone?"

"No, Toni! We put you where we need you."

"But I'm not being challenged enough with these assignments that you're giving me. I need to be challenged more. I can handle more dangerous assignments. I've been highly trained, for what? I need to be utilized more for overseas assignments. And I speak seven languages and don't even get to use four of them."

"Maybe next time."

Toni was tired of trying to beat around the bush.

"What about Italy?"

Tom stared at Toni; stone faced.

"What *about* Italy?"

Toni decided to play it off.

"Well, anywhere in Europe. Or the Middle East. Or Asia. Somewhere. Anywhere other than the states."

She was hoping that mentioning Italy would help him to consider her for the *job*. She was also hoping that he wasn't all of a sudden developing a fatherly concern for her welfare. At this point, it was too late, in her opinion. She was about to come clean about listening in on the conversation.

"Didn't I overhear you and Felix mentioning a job in Italy?"

"Now how would that have happened?"

"Didn't one of you mention it while I was here yesterday?"

"Toni, did you bug my office?"

Toni had the stupid look on her face but wouldn't look at Tom. She started fidgeting on his desk.

"TONI!!!" Tom shouted her name like a father scolding his disobedient child.

"WHAT???" Toni shouts back with the same tone and vigor.

"You heard what I said, young lady! Did you bug my office?"

"Well, I think I dropped something in your trash, by accident." Toni sheepishly gives Tom the *It wasn't intentional* side eye.

"I'm very disappointed in you! You know that is a reprehensible offense. You should be suspended with plans to terminate."

"Yeah, but we both know that in this business, termination really means, *termination*."

Tom looks over at his hard-headed, new-found daughter and wants to put her over his lap and spank her for putting herself in a potentially career altering position.

"Just give me the assignment! I can handle it!"

Tom isn't so sure.

"Look! Stop looking at me as your daughter. That's irrelevant in this business. And at this point, it's *really* irrelevant. Also, no one should know, because it will leave you in danger."

Tom laughs. "It'll leave *me* in danger?" He laughs again.

"Yeah, you. I can take care of myself."

"Oh, and I can't?"

"You're getting old. I'm sure that you've slowed down."

Tom *truly* wants to spank her now.

"Well, you're quite wrong. I can still handle the best of them. Skill over speed at this point is all I need. And it's what I have."

"Okay, then you have no reason to deny me the job."

Tom realized that the Italian target was actually the same one connected to the Chicago assignment that Toni identified. He gave her the full speech about the danger she would be in. He broke down every step of danger that she would be facing. This is what Toni wanted. It's what she needed to prove herself as a highly skilled agent.

"Alright! I'll let Felix know that I chose you for the assignment. But Toni, please don't make me regret this. Even though I just found out that you're my daughter... I do want to have some type of real relationship with you. That's something that I never thought I would ever have.

"I won't!"

Tom let Felix know that he chose Toni as his choice for Italy and that he would put someone else on her original assignment. Felix was satisfied with Tom's choice.

## Italia

*Milan.*

Toni was on her way to Italy, and she was anxious for this assignment to play out. The biggest challenge would be to make it back home by way of something other than a casket. She knew the risk and it excited her more than frightened her. "Forewarned is forearmed" is the quote that kept coming to mind. She chose the assignment. She knew the danger she was facing. This was also her chance to use all the skills she had acquired and prove herself one of the best spies in the agency.

Milan is one of the top fashion hubs in the world and Toni loved fashion. She was often mistaken for a model with her height and fitness, although she was curvier than the average model. For this assignment, Toni had to cut off her beautiful coils. Her hair was cut extremely short and close to her head. She bleached it blonde for a more exotic look. She also had to lose 25 pounds in order to lose most of her curves. The target liked his women boyish slim. She would miss her natural hair that she came to love, and her curves that Yusuf couldn't keep his eyes and hands off of.

The target was a rich Italian fashion baron who had lived in the U.S. for years. He fled the U.S. after supplying the Italian mafia with military arms from the states. He was almost caught but managed to slip out of the country in a private jet when he found out the government was gathering information that would make him a target for arrest. The information initiated by Toni as she uncovered it during the Chicago operation.

He had a weakness for model types of any nationality. Toni was characterized as, of African American and Italian heritage. She also spoke fluent Italian and would play up her Italian *side* for this assignment.

Her assignment was to befriend Giovanni, as a former model who owned a successful women's retail clothing store in the U.S. She was to get close enough to him so that she would be able to allow American agents to arrest him and take him back to the U.S. under the radar of the Italian government. They were unwilling to give him up even though they had an extradition treaty with the U.S.

The agency knew that the odds were against Toni. If Giovanni didn't kill her, his people probably would, or the Italian mafia, or the Italian government. They just needed her to get as close to him as possible, in order for them to move in on him and arrest him.

Another reason the U.S. government wanted him was because there were five missing women who were involved with Giovanni. All were his lovers, but none were found. He was a known misogynist and finally identified as a probable serial killer. He may have killed more women in other states and countries. Toni had her hands full with this assignment and her life was in jeopardy from many different angles.

*Giovanni Romero.*

Toni showed up at a fashion event that Giovanni was hosting. Her connections got her on the guest list. She studied Giovanni well before she left the states. She was still reading up on him on the flight in. She knew exactly what he liked in women. She made sure she wore one of his sexiest designs. His narcissism would never allow him to ignore a beautiful woman wearing one of his favorite creations. He sent one of his people to bring her over to meet him. She obliged.

Giovanni was a short, unattractive, 40 something year old man, with a dark tan, well-groomed black hair, and a fully shaven face. He was well dressed in a beautiful cobalt blue European cut suit, with cognac shoes and a cognac belt. His style made up for his physical shortcomings.

"Giovanni Romero... Toni Brice..." Said one of his bodyguards.


*** (All conversation between Toni and Giovanni are in Italian.)

"My you're beautiful! Are you a model, dear?"

"I'm very honored to meet you sir." Toni extended her hand.

"Nonsense!" Giovanni grabbed her hand and pulled her into a hug instead of a handshake.

"None of that handshake trifle from such a lovely lady."

Toni smiled.

"So... are you... a model?"

"No, Mr. Romero—"

"Ah AHHHH, Giovanni. Or Gio."

"My apologies. No, Giovanni! I gave up modeling years ago. I now own my own women's clothing business."

"That's wonderful! Do you carry any of my collections?"

"Yes, I do! It's one of my favorites, as you can see." Toni spins around to give him the full effect of herself in his creation.

"Beautiful! Just, beautiful! I hope that you're able to join us in my suite a little later. A private get together for a few of my friends. Please join us. Are you alone or did you come with friends?"

"I came alone."

"Perfect. I would've invited your friends too if you came with some. But since it's just you, I welcome your presence."

"Thank you! I appreciate such a distinguished invitation. I'm honored!"

While Toni was talking to Giovanni, she saw Mateo on the other side of the room; he winked at her. She was excited to see him. He was a collaborating agent with U.S. intelligence, so he helped out the U.S. when they called on his agency; especially in the European region. He flew to Milan from Barcelona to be an ally for Toni when she needed him.

When he saw her, she was as sexy as ever and he loved her new look. A little skinny for him, but the look turned him on, none the less. He gestured for her to meet him outside of the room. She made her excuses to Giovanni as she checked her phone.

"Please excuse me. I have to make a phone call."

Giovanni gave a slight nod of approval, then engaged in conversation with some other guests.

Toni left the room and looked for Mateo. She saw him waiting for her in the lobby. They walked to a side hallway.

"Toni, et veus absolutament expquisit! Us necessito ARA, el meu amor!" * (In Catalan)

(Translation - "Toni, you look absolutely exquisite! I need you NOW, my love!")

"Ja saps que és massa perillós, Mateo. Per a tots dos." Said Toni.

(Translaton - "You know that it's too dangerous, Mateo. For both of us." Said Toni.)

"Això és el que fa que sigui tan emocionant, el meu amor."

(Translation - "That's what makes it so exciting, my love.")

Toni agreed. She told him to meet her in the lady's room in about 30 minutes. She went back into the room as to not draw too much suspicion. She walked over to Giovanni for a few minutes while he was talking to a few guests. She joined in on the conversation long enough to have to check her phone again. She then told him that she had to make another call and use the restroom.

As she entered the restroom it was pretty quiet. It seemed empty, but she didn't want to call out Mateo's name just in case there was someone else in there. Mateo entered a stall so that no one would report him for being in there. Toni stood back far enough to be able to look under the stalls without stooping. She was looking for men's shoes. She found them.

"Obre l'amor." She whispered.

(Translation - "Open up love.") She whispered.

Mateo was at the far end stall. He opened up and pulled her in. They began kissing and hugging and tugging at each other's clothes right away. Toni had on a dress, so it was easy access for Mateo. He spun her around and had her put her hands up on the wall over the toilet. He pulled up her dress and kissed and licked up her back, as his hands cupped her breasts after he pushed her bra over them.

He managed to get his pants down far enough to release himself. He pushed himself inside of Toni from the back and aggressively had his way with her. The entire episode was exciting for her and caused her to orgasm quickly and intensely. Quickies were always invigorating to her.

"Mmm…, gràcies per això, Amor!" Said Toni.

("Mmm…, thank you for that, Love!" Said Toni.)

"No gràcies!"

("No, thank you!")

They gave each other a quick kiss on the lips. She knew that she had to get back to Giovanni, so she pulled herself together quickly. She left first just in case someone was watching her. Mateo stayed behind until he felt Toni was back with Giovanni. He couldn't leave when he was ready because a couple of females entered the bathroom before he could get out. He sat on the toilet and checked some text messages until he was sure that he was alone again. He then had the chance to leave without anyone seeing him in the lady's room.

Once they all got to Giovanni's suite, he had Toni sit right next to him. He wanted to talk fashion with her.

"What is the name of your business?" Said Giovanni.

This was all covered by the agency. As part of the preparation for the assignment, they had bought out a high-end clothing store that carried his brands in Rittenhouse Square in Philadelphia. Toni was penned as the owner and the paperwork made it seem as if she were a silent partner for all the years the former owner had it, until she bought her out. She then became, and is now, the sole owner of the fashion boutique.

"Boutique Di Moda in Piazza."

"I love the name. Which of my lines do you have displayed at this time?"

"Your Gia line!"

"Bravissimo!"

("Very Good!")

Toni researched and studied his fashion line before coming to Italy. She really did have the line featured in the store. And she knew every piece that was a part of it. Giovanni was quite impressed with her knowledge of the fashions, the fabrics and the colors that highlighted the clothing line.

She asked about his newest line and he couldn't contain his excitement to tell her. He asked her to consider being in his fashion show. She said that she would consider it but knew that she wouldn't. She had never walked a runway before and to attempt it for his fashion show would blow her cover as a former model.

Giovanni was very attracted to Toni. But he was also a cunning predator, so he would never try to move in on her so soon. He needed to check her out before pulling her into his world. She was new meat for him. He ran through a new woman every six months. He always had more than one and never hid it. He didn't have to. He was "Giovanni Romero!"

### Sadist or Masochist?

It's getting closer to the 6 months mark. Giovanni has been getting more and more aggressive with Toni during sex. He has become more distant with her socially and intimately. Even though they have sex often, it was getting cold and impersonal. He hardly kissed or cuddled anymore. Toni knows that he is going to make his move towards making her another victim. She knows to be on guard, or she can lose her life.

Giovanni is stressed about some business matters. Toni has listened and poked around enough to know that it had to do with the arms business. He was unable to fulfill a contract. His connections in the U.S. were being watched so they couldn't move the merchandise. His buyer couldn't have cared less. That wasn't any of his concern. He expects his merchandise, or their will be consequences for Giovanni and his entire organization.

He wants to see Toni and has one of his limo drivers pick her up at the villa and bring her to the condo. She can see that he's stressed.

"We're going to have dinner in the bedroom, dear." Says Giovanni.

"Okay! I'll wait for you in there."

Giovanni had company in the living room and was talking business, so Toni didn't want to seem too nosey. She was playing the obedient girlfriend, although she had previously placed practically undetectable bugs in several spots in the condo, and the agency could hear almost everything that's being said. He's trying to find another supplier for the deal he committed to. Once his company left, he came into the bedroom pretty wound up. His mood was tense.

"Get your clothes off!"

"I thought we were having dinner, babe?"

"FUCK dinner! Now take your fucking clothes off!"

"Why are you talking to me like that? I'm not taking anything off!"

"BITCH! … Take your fucking clothes off or I'll cut them off of you!"

Toni had to continue to play the frightened girlfriend until she got the information she needed. She had to find out about the missing girls, and she needed to find an in for the agents to capture Giovanni with the least number of casualties and to do it without the Italian government knowing about it.

Toni took off her clothes but kept her underwear on.

"No no no no no… Take EVERYTHING off!"

She had to invoke her acting training that her parents signed her up for when she was a young girl and teenager. So, she acted sad and frightened but thought about how he must've treated the missing women. It was hard for her not to say what she wanted and do what she wanted.

She removed her underwear. Now she was completely nude. She was about to sit on the bed.

"Stand up and turn around."

She did what she was told. Giovanni put handcuffs on her wrists in back of her. He made them tight.

"They're too tight, Gio!"

"Shut the fuck up! That's how I want them."

She quieted herself but had to keep telling herself that it was all necessary.

"Now turn around and get the fuck on your knees."

She did as she was told. He was nude as he stood in front of her with his erection in her face. He pulled his gun from his dresser and put it to her head. Toni was very much on edge and tried to pay attention to his movements and the tiniest sounds of the gun.

"I want you to suck it you dirty bitch."

She was used to his degrading words and knew that she had to accept them for the assignment. She followed his command.

"Now, I want you to use your teeth as my cock goes in and out of your mouth."

Toni gladly used her teeth but wanted to bite it off.

"No, I need your teeth to scrape my cock until it bleeds. And you better not even think about biting it. If you do, I'll splatter your brains on the wall."

Toni wasn't sure if he really wanted her to do it or if he just needed a reason to kill her. This was becoming a masochistic episode. Not just his usual sadistic shit. She was on edge, but she clamped her teeth at the base of his penis and slowly pulled them to his tip. He tilted his head towards the ceiling and hollered. The barrel of the gun was still on her head. All she could do was fantasize about using her skills to pull back away from the gun, knee him in the balls, then head butt him into unconsciousness. She knew how to get out of the handcuffs.

She tried to keep her focus on his every motion to try to figure out where he was going with this. He wasn't bleeding yet, so he told her to do it again. She did it again. It seemed to be getting raw, but no blood yet.

"Keep doing it until it bleeds, you dirty bitch!"

Toni was super pissed off. This made it a bit easier to do, although she just wanted to separate him from his member.

Toni did it twice more, then she could taste the blood.

"Yes! Yes! Now suck the blood off it without using your teeth. Suck it good."

All she could think about at that moment was how glad she was that she collected enough semen to be tested by the agency for HIV. She was also given an anti-viral to prevent any viruses, just in case. The government had a prevention for AIDS that was not available to the people. This wasn't unusual.

So, Toni nauseously sucked it until he told her to stop.

"Now, clamp your teeth down at the base of my balls. Use your teeth as you pull them over my balls. Keep doing it until you draw blood."

Toni was done with all this and didn't want to go any further. She took too long to follow his directions, so Giovanni slammed the gun into her face.

"Bitch do as you are told! Now clamp your teeth at the base of my balls!"

Toni did as he told her to do until she could figure her way out of this, without compromising her ability to find out about the missing girls. He screamed each time she did it. It took her three times to draw blood.

"Now lick the blood off my balls."

As she was trying not to vomit, she managed to get the blood off of him. Giovanni then walked behind her, grabbed her by the handcuffs, then threw her on the bed on her stomach…

-----

*Where's Giovanni?*

The night had passed and now it was morning. Giovanni's bodyguards hadn't heard from him for 12 hours now. This was highly unusual. One of the guards contacted his personal assistant. His condo was right next door, so he was their immediately. He knocked on the bedroom door.

"Mr. Romero?"

There was a 30 second pause then he banged on the bedroom door several times.

"Mr. Romero, sir?" There was no response. His assistant told the guard to call the other guards into the room.

"I've banged on the door several times with no answer. I need one of you to kick it in. I'm not sure what we're going to find so I need you all to be ready for anything."

All 6 guards pulled their guns out, almost synchronously. They all got into a formation. The guard in the front kicked the door in. There was no Giovanni. The room was empty.

The police were called once the guards checked the room out and removed any type of incriminating evidence. As the police scoured the room for answers, they found small amounts of blood and other DNA. They would secure it all as evidence. The police were told by Giovanni's personal assistant that he was in the room with Toni. They gave all the information they had on her. They were unable to locate her or Giovanni.

As the days passed, there was a hit put out on his life because he did not make the deal that he had entered into. The belief was that he fled the country because of this. But the people closest to him knew better. He would never leave alone and without his personal assistant and bodyguards. They knew that somehow Toni was involved with his disappearance. They would use all of their resources to find out who Toni Brice really was, and what happened                to                Giovanni.

# Job Not Well Done

*Toni's Back.*

Toni walked into Tom's office and Felix was there too. She had bruises on her face and head.

"How are you Toni?" Said Felix.

"I'm fine, sir."

Toni slammed a piece of paper on the desk.

"Here is a list of 10 names of women the target killed, whose names he could remember. 10 places he buried these victims and more. He couldn't remember any more names or places, although he admitted there were more."

"Where is he?" Said Felix.

"He's dead sir." Said Toni.

"*And why is he dead*!" Shouted Felix. "The assignment was to give us an in, so that we could come collect him and bring him back to the states. Why is the target dead?"

"We couldn't preserve his life. It was unable to be helped."

"Really?" Felix responded with an "I don't believe you" tone and expression.

"Where is his body, Toni?"

"We had to dispose of it."

Felix was visibly angry. He gestured for Tom to follow him to his office. When Tom got back, he let Toni know that she was out of order. And that she didn't stick to the plan. He needed to know where the body was. She told Tom exactly the events as they happened.

-----

Meanwhile, back in Milan, a body washes up on a beach. A group of young adults find it as they run towards the water about to go for a swim. It has duct tape wrapped around the bottom half of its face. When the police and coroner arrive, the coroner cuts the tape to find out who it might be. Once the tape is cut, they find something shoved in the deceased's mouth. They identify it as male genitalia. And as they check the rest of the body, they conclude that it's his own genitalia missing from where it should be. His penis was shoved as far down his throat as it could go, and his testicles were stuffed in his mouth.

Word on the street was that he entered into a deal he wasn't able to deliver on. So, it was assumed that this was the payback for not delivering.

-----

Toni explained to Tom how it all went down—

After Giovanni grabbed her handcuffs and threw her on the bed, he attempted to shove himself into her anus. As this was happening, Mateo came out of the closet and hit Giovanni on the head with a slap jack and knocked him out. He then drugged him with a tranquilizer, hypodermically. They were able to get him out through his closet.

Mateo rented the condo next to Giovanni's (on the opposite side from where his personal assistant lived). The bedroom closets of both were attached. Mateo had the entire adjacent closet wall removed and reattached as a movable wall. So, when Giovanni was unconscious, they were able to take him out of the bedroom, through the closet, then remove the wall to get him into the condo next door. The wall was put back in place without an easily visible way to tell that it was movable. All of the seams met perfectly, with locks in place on Mateo's side of the wall.

After getting him into the condo next door, they put him into a dresser that Mateo had made to carry out two bodies. Giovanni's and Toni's. They were carried out down the back stairwell by a moving company. Well, a pretend moving company. They were driven to a garage about 15 minutes away, then the dresser with Giovanni still in it was transferred to a van.

Toni got out and sat in the back of the van next to the dresser. It still wasn't safe for her to be seen. Another 30 minutes away, Mateo rented a car for Toni to drive herself to Barcelona. It was about a 10-hour drive as she followed Mateo in the van. They had to make a couple of stops along the way. During each stop they tranquilized Giovanni to keep him unconscious.

Once they got to Mateo's Catalunya villa, he had a couple of guys waiting to help him with the dresser. Toni pulled up and went into the villa after them. Before Giovanni's tranquilizer wore off, he was tied up on a chair in the basement of the villa.

Toni couldn't wait to question him. She knew that he would be difficult, so she had her torturous plans to make him talk.

He continued to be difficult even after Toni would hit him in his face several times. She then thought about what he did to her, grabbed his testicles and cut them off with a straight blade in one quick swipe. Giovanni screamed from the pain as he was bleeding heavily onto the floor.

"What did you do with Audra Marie's body? Your last girlfriend when you were still in the states. We know that you killed her. Where is her body?"

Giovanni continued to cry and moan from the pain and loss of his testicles, with no answer for Toni.

"If you don't tell me *right now*... what you did with Audra Marie's body... I will cut your mother fucking dick off! You get this one last time to answer my question. Where is Audra Marie's body?"

He's still crying and moaning so Toni lifts her hand and straight razor in the air, then...

"She's buried on the hill!!!"

Giovanni screams his answer fearing that Toni was ready to separate him from his penis.

"What hill?" Asks Toni.

Giovanni thinks that he's bought some time with his partial answer, but Toni is getting impatient. She slices into the base of his penis, just enough to let him know that he's only a second from losing his member.

He screams the answer. Toni continues to grill him about all of the missing women that he's connected to. He slowly cries out what he can remember, as Toni records the information on her phone's audio recorder.

He then gave her all the information she asked for that he could remember. What she received wasn't sufficient enough, because every – single – female – who he killed was important to her. But she knew that he would probably start hallucinating from the pain and losing so much blood; or making things up, in order to end the questioning. She left him there in pain to think about all the women he tortured and killed; she hoped that he'd bleed to death.

All of a sudden, she remembered the men and boys who raped her as a child. This was a chance to get revenge on them all. She had a transference of revenge onto Giovanni. She cut off his penis and threw it on the floor. She left him there to bleed out. She went up to talk to Mateo and had him listen to all that he confessed to.

Once she got back downstairs, he was dead. She picked up his penis off the floor then shoved it down his throat. She then grabbed his testicles out of the bloody mass it laid in on the floor, then stuffed them in his mouth. She walked over to Mateo's tool station and grabbed some duct tape. She wrapped the bottom of his face up with it so that his genitals remained in place.

Toni let Mateo know that he could come and get rid of the body. He threw a tarp on the floor, away from the blood, then threw his body onto it. He then wrapped it up tightly, threw it over his shoulder, then threw it in the van. He got rid of the body that night.

*Closure.*

"Ten women's bodies were found. We were able to give closure to all of those families, so in spite of your shortcomings within the assignment, this is major. You can be very proud of that, Toni."

Tom had just gotten a report back from the FBI about the missing girls. This gave Toni a feeling of accomplishment. This helped to make her feel as though she had made a difference.

After her debriefing, the agency ordered Toni to therapy, considering the gruesome end to her last assignment. Not because they were worried about her actions, but because they wanted to make sure that she wasn't going to be negatively affected by them. Her psychiatrist wanted to make sure that her skills to cope with her actions following the assignment were adequate. She also gave her some added skills to help prevent any post traumatic episodes.

Toni was armed with all she needed to handle the possible emotional repercussions of her actions. She was good with what she did and balanced the psychopathology of her behavior, with the reasons her actions were implemented.

Once she completed the agencies stipulations, she was off to vacation for the next four weeks. She was ready for her down time in Rio de Janeiro, but was Brazil ready for Toni?

#WhosToniRice???

**Lisa A. Forrest** is a writer whose first novel **Parlons Café**
was published in February of 2018.
This is her second fictional novel with many more on the way.
She lives on the outskirts of her hometown
of Philadelphia, PA, in Boothwyn, PA.


You can follow her blogs at:

www.therealfountainofyouth.family

&

Her Parlons Café Facebook page at:

https://www.facebook.com/lisaaforrest2018/

www.ingramcontent.com/pod-product-compliance
Lightning Source LLC
Chambersburg PA
CBHW021458250626
47154CB00004BA/1336